KT-177-077

The Stolen

Alex Shearer lives with his family in Somerset. He has two children. He has written more than a dozen books for both adults and children, as well as many successful television series, films and stage and radio plays. He has had over thirty different jobs, and has never given up trying to play the guitar.

Praise for The Stolen

'Alex Shearer is fascinated by states of existence, both spiritual and earthbound; but he's also an excellent storyteller; and this one has a nail-biting twist'
Mail on Sunday

'A cracking plot . . . a thrillingly unexpected twist'
The Sunday Telegraph

'A startlingly imaginative tale . . . this is a split-level book: read it literally as fantasy or as a thoughtful account of how elderly people are treated, and how they feel'
The Independent Magazine

'A dark, atmospheric tale'
The Herald

Praise for The Great Blue Yonder

'A sensitive, gentle exploration of the saddest thing that can ever happen . . . very moving indeed'
The Times

'This is book of the year for me – and I don't think a child over the age of nine could fail to be smitten'
Sunday Telegraph

Also by Alex Shearer

The Great Blue Yonder
The Speed of the Dark

The Stolen

Alex Shearer

MACMILLAN CHILDREN'S BOOKS

First published 2002 by Macmillan Children's Books

This edition published 2003 by Macmillan Children's Books
a division of Macmillan Publishers Limited
20 New Wharf Road, London N1 9RR
Basingstoke and Oxford
www.panmacmillan.com

Associated companies throughout the world

ISBN 0 330 39892 X

Text copyright © Alex Shearer 2002

The right of Alex Shearer to be identified as the
author of this work has been asserted by him in accordance
with the Copyright, Designs and Patents Act 1988.

1 3 5 7 9 8 6 4 2

A CIP catalogue record for this book is available from
the British Library.

Phototypeset by Intype London Ltd
Printed and bound in Great Britain by Mackays of Chatham plc, Kent

Contents

I

To Begin at the Middle

The first thing you have to know is that I didn't have any brothers or sisters and there was no one to please but myself. Which was just fine. Most of the time. The rest of the time it wasn't, necessarily, though even then it wasn't too bad. It was only sometimes when it all got as dry as dust, and there were too many adults about that I wished there was someone else there my age too.

I don't know if you ever get that feeling – that fusty mothballs feeling. It's the feeling you get when the little specks of dust hang in the sunlight and the whole empty afternoon is before you, like a desert, with nothing to do and nowhere to go and nobody coming round.

Your mum says to play in the garden, but somehow even the thought of it just makes you tired. And even if you went out and played tennis against the wall, you'd only whack the ball into next door's garden, and then have to knock on the door and get stung by all the nettles round the back. The only way to make things better is to have another world to escape into. But who knows where it is? Or how you would get to it, anyway. And so you just drift and dream, as if your mind was on a magic carpet and you had left your body far away in another land. So maybe you do escape, in a way.

Which is what I want to tell you about – about escaping.

There being only me to please, I'd probably gone a bit bonkers. I dare say I was a bit selfish too, and liked to have everything my own way and just so. I'd probably got more stuff than most people and I never played with half of it. I just kept it in the cupboard and I didn't like anyone touching it, or disturbing my straight lines. And woe betide you if you did.

I think I was what they call eccentric. I don't suppose my hair helps either, it being extremely red, and then there's my freckles, which aren't red, but there are a lot of them. They can get quite bad in the summer and I look like a packet of cornflakes with a hat on.

Sometimes I wished I had a sister, but other times I didn't. I've seen people with sisters and they don't always get on so well. They're often quarrelling over what belongs to who and accusing each other of pinching things. But then other times, when things go wrong, you've always got somebody to tell you that things aren't so bad. I know that your mum or dad can also do this, but it's not the same, because sometimes *they're* the problem. It's having someone your own age – I mean, someone who understands, not someone who has forgotten, or who cannot imagine now, or who never knew anyway. It's not always someone grown-up and old you want to talk to, it's someone young.

And that's the other thing I want to tell you about

as well. About being young, and not being young, especially not being young when you ought to be. (I know that doesn't make much sense yet, but it will do later. At least I hope so.)

What I'm really saying is that the worst thing you can ever steal from anybody, to my mind, is their time. I hate it when people steal your time, or waste it, or bore you solid. It's all right to waste your own time, because after all, it belongs to you. But it's not really anyone else's. So many other things can be replaced. Even if someone stole all your money, you might get it back again or make some more. But if somebody steals your time, what can you do about that? Time passes and it's gone. It's the most valuable thing you can ever have. There's no going back. There's no getting some more from somewhere. There's no borrowing some from somebody else. At least not unless you're—

Well, that's part of it too.

Because there was just me and I was on my own quite often and had to talk to grown-ups a lot as there was nobody sensible to talk to, or maybe because I usually had my nose in a book a lot of the time, people sometimes said that I was 'old beyond my years' or that I'd got 'an old head on young shoulders'. It seemed a funny sort of thing to say, but they did. Or they'd say to you that you were growing up too fast, as if you were in charge of a bicycle, and had some sort of control over how fast you were pedalling on your way to growing up.

But this idea of an old head on young shoulders is important too. Because that's all part of it as well, though in a different way. It was never that straight-forward, as so many things are. All they ever get to be is complicated, at least that's my experience, such as it is.

Which leads me on to grannies.

Personally I'd always been very interested in grannies, due to not really having one myself. Both my grannies died before I was born, so I felt that I'd missed out on them and should have been entitled to one, or at least have been able to rent one from some-where. A nice neat and tidy one, with a big hat and a handbag.

In my daydreams I used to have a granny who would take me to places I never usually went to, and buy me more sweets than were good for either of us. We'd go to the zoo to look at the animals and my granny would say, 'Just fancy', when we looked at the baboons and their big red bottoms. Then we'd have ice creams afterwards as well and say, 'It's only once in a lifetime'. And then we'd go back and do the same thing again next week. Or maybe try somewhere else.

She'd have white hair, dyed slightly blue, or maybe lavender, and I'd tell her what had happened to me during the week and she'd pretend to be ever so inter-ested and say, 'Yes, dear', but all the time she would only really be looking round for a bench to sit on.

Sometimes I used to wonder why you couldn't get a game called Virtual Granny that you could install on the computer, and then you could have a granny whenever you wanted, at the click of a mouse.

Anyway, there I was, granny-less. I guess I was mostly on my own. But I wasn't lonely, except for now and again. And I think that everyone is lonely

4

sometimes, even when they're surrounded by all their friends. I think that these lonely moments just come over you sometimes, and there's nothing you can do about them but wait for them to go away. Sometimes I think that being lonely is like that.

I suppose it all seems all jumbled up now and doesn't make any sense at all. My mum is always saying that to me: 'Begin at the beginning, Carly,' she says. 'Don't go all round the houses! Begin at the beginning! Just tell me what happened.' (My real name is Scarlet, not Carly, but I changed it on the grounds that it's quite enough having hair and freckles without drawing everyone's attention to the fact.)

Mrs Chardwick used to say the same about my English, about going round the houses. But to be honest, I like going round the houses. And as for beginning at the beginning, the reason I never start there is that I don't know where the beginning is, and that's the honest truth. And anyway, I've never known anything in my whole life that ever started at the beginning. Things aren't like that. They usually start about halfway through, or near the end, and then work their way backwards, that's how most things are.

But I promise that although I'm not very good at beginnings I'll try to organize things so that it all makes sense in the end. And as long as you can get the end right, maybe the beginning doesn't matter so much, just as long as you manage to get started.

One last thing I ought to say is that although I'm on my own now, I did have a sister once, for a little while, only that was back when I was small and she was even smaller. She was born too soon and tiny as a doll, and they kept her warm in an incubator. And her name was Marsha. But she wasn't very strong and she slept all the time, and after a while she never woke up. Mum and Dad were sad, and so was I, because I'd wanted a sister and I did have one for a while. But it was really only for a moment, and then I didn't any more.

Sometimes I had dreams about my sister who never grew up. Sometimes we fought and sometimes we were friends, but we were always together. And if anyone picked on her or called her names I'd call them names right back, and I'd hold her hand as we crossed the road and give her half my chocolate. Then I'd tell her all I knew about the world, as I'd done things first and been in it longer, and I'd have been her big sister. I'd have looked after her better than anyone, and we'd both have been all right.

2

Meredith

So anyway, that's me and here I am. To be honest, I could talk about myself all day, given half the chance or even a quarter. I know it's a bad habit and you shouldn't really, but I think that it's just nerves. Or it was then. Of course, I'm different now, after all my experiences, which can only be good for a person, though Mum doesn't believe a word of some of the things I say. And when I try to tell her she says, 'Now, Carly!' and tries to be stern. But what's the use in being stern when what's true is true and being stern isn't going to change it?

Most playtimes before it all happened I would be on my own in a corner somewhere, just me and my freckles, trying to stay out of the sun to stop them spreading. Freckles are a bit like exotic plants and they grow like mad in the sunlight. You can start off with one, go out into the sunshine, and the next time you look into the mirror, you're covered in them. They even start to join up until you're nothing but a freckle, one great big, walking freckle with hair on top.

Although I was on my own a lot, I did have friends and you don't have to feel sorry for me as I'm not expecting sympathy or even asking for it. But I didn't have a special friend, not like some people did, and I did wish I had one, though even in wishing I had one, I didn't really know if I wanted one or not.

Friends are like pets, Mum says. She doesn't mean you have to muck them out and feed them lettuce, but she says you have to look after them and pay attention to them and take an interest in them and make sure that they never feel neglected. Sometimes I felt a special friend would be a big responsibility and I'd never be able to look after her properly. That was why I reckoned a sister might be better. Because I'd seen girls with sisters and, according to them, you can be as nasty as you like, and even give them a good punching every now and again – not that I'm saying that you should, only that you could if you wanted to. And no matter what you do to them, they still have to go home with you. And so even if you hate each other sometimes, at least you're never lonely and you always have somebody to argue with. Because blood is thicker than water, as people say. (But then so is ketchup.)

So that was what I wanted really, a sort of best-friend sister – someone who wouldn't mind or be offended if I had an off-day; someone who would forgive me if I wasn't always nice. And I'd forgive them too, of course, if they weren't nice to me. No one can be perfect all the time. That's what I think.

So I was always on the look-out for new people who I could maybe make special friends with, new girls who might turn up halfway through the term, or maybe at the start of a new school year. There were always a few of those at our school. Their mums or dads would have moved to the neighbourhood for new jobs and things, or maybe it was because they hadn't got on so well at another school. There could be all sorts of reasons.

Anyway, it was September – a new term and a new school year. There didn't seem to be any new pupils in our class at first, but then after a couple of days Meredith turned up. Her granny brought her along. She was a very old, very slow sort of granny, not a lively one at all. She walked along as though she needed somebody to lean on, or someone to oil her knees.

The teacher introduced Meredith to us and we all said hello and that we were pleased to see her – though if she hadn't turned up we probably wouldn't have been that bothered because, as my dad says, what you've never had you don't miss.

Anyway, I sat and I watched Meredith for a while as the lesson wore on, and I started to wonder if maybe she couldn't be the best friend I had been waiting for. There were things about her which just made her seem right, really. I mean, she didn't have freckles, not like I had, but all the same she seemed a bit apart from everyone else, the way I feel sometimes. Maybe everyone feels like that but nobody talks about it. And if nobody ever talks about something, how do you know?

Well, at break-time a lot of people made an effort to be friendly to Meredith, and they tried to have a chat with her, or they invited her to join in a game. But although she was equally polite and friendly back, she didn't join in anything.

'Thank you very much for asking,' I heard her say. 'That's very kind of you. But I think I'll decline for the moment, if that's all right. I'd prefer to read my book.'

And so Rona Gusket, who had asked Meredith if she wanted to play hopscotch, and Dave Hobbs, who had asked her if she wanted to do some mud wrestling, both edged away, giving her funny looks, maybe feeling a little bit rebuffed and rejected.

Yet she hadn't been rude. It was just one of those firm refusals.

But there was something odd about the way she had spoken. *'I think I'll decline for the moment.'* It didn't sound like something you'd usually say. It sounded – I don't know – somehow too *old*. Too old for Meredith, that was. I mean, if her granny had said something like, 'I think I'll decline,' you'd have thought that was just granny-speak. But maybe Meredith had heard her granny use that expression once and it had rubbed off on her. Maybe that was it.

So break-time went on. People tried to be friendly with Meredith and they just as quickly gave up on her. If she wanted to be left alone, that was her business. If she wanted to join in, she was welcome to. If she didn't, well, nobody was going to ask her twice, or feel obliged to persuade her.

I don't know if Meredith knew that I was watching her from the far corner of the playground that day. I suspect – knowing what I do now – that she was, that the whole thing was planned in advance, that she had her eye out for a lonely, sort of solitary, sort of freckly girl. Maybe not. Maybe that's just the 'benefit of hindsight' as Mrs Chardwick says. Maybe that's just me being wise after the event.

But let's face it, I wasn't very wise before it.

As I watched Meredith that morning, I realized what it was that separated her from all the other children. It wasn't her height – although she was fairly tall, not the tallest in the playground, but taller than most of us – and it wasn't her face (she was pretty), or her complexion (fair), or her hair (brown), or her clothes (nice enough), or anything at all like that. It was something else. She just looked so utterly and completely bored, and every few minutes she would look from her book to her wrist-watch, glance at the time and sigh heavily as if to say, 'Is that *all* the time that's passed since I last looked?', before going back to her book again.

Now I get bored sometimes. Everyone does. But it's lessons I get bored with, not playtime. But Meredith's boredom seemed to run deeper even than lessons or playtime or long car journeys or wet summer holidays when there's nothing to do. Her boredom ran deeper than traffic jams and deeper than your mum's conversations with people in the supermarket who she hasn't seen for years. Meredith just seemed totally bored with *everything*. She looked around the playground, at the games of football, hopscotch and all the rest, and her lip seemed to curl with disdain at such trivial activities. She just simply didn't have the time for it. 'How could you!' her expression seemed to say. 'How *tedious* it all is.'

And then she looked at her watch again and sighed – the way I imagine a prisoner locked in a cell might sigh, a prisoner with a long, long sentence to serve, who shudders at the thought of all the time that has yet to pass before she can be free. She shudders and wishes it could all be over, in the blink of an eye.

11

'Hi,' I said. 'I'm Carly.'

Meredith looked up from her book. I can't remember what she was reading, but it wasn't a book I knew. It looked a bit like a grown-up book, about grown-up things, the kind of grown-up things which are completely boring, until you're *maybe* grown up yourself.

'Hi, Carly,' she said, pleasantly enough, forcing herself to give me a small smile. 'How are you?'

'Fine,' I said. 'And you?'

'Fine,' she answered. 'Thank you. Just fine.'

She glanced at her book again, almost as if to say, 'You can go now. You're dismissed.'

But I'm not so easy to get rid of.

'You're new then, are you?' I said – just for the sake of conversation. I knew that she was new and she knew that she was new too. Neither of us needed to say it, but I said it anyway.

'Yes,' she nodded. 'I am.'

'Where are you from?' I asked. (I'm not really nosy, just a bit curious sometimes.)

'Easton,' she said.

'Oh,' I said. It meant nothing to me. 'Where's that, then?'

'Miles away,' she said. 'Miles and miles. A long way from here.'

She turned a page of her book, but I didn't go away. I still hadn't given up on her yet as a possible best-friend-in-waiting.

'So what did you move for?' I asked – and I probably *was* being a bit nosy by then.

'Personal reasons,' she said.

'Did you move for your dad's job?' I persisted.

'I haven't got a dad,' she said. But she didn't exactly seem sad about it, just matter-of-fact,

'Mum's job, then?' I said.

'I don't have a mum either,' she answered. 'Not any more.'

'What happened to them?' I asked.

'They were lost,' she said, 'in a bad accident, at sea.'

'Oh,' I said. 'I'm sorry.' (I felt a bit shocked, actually, and didn't know what else to say.)

'It was a long time ago,' Meredith said, and then she gave a small, sad smile. 'I'm over the worst of it now.'

'Got any special friends?' I asked her. 'I bet you'd probably need some special friends if you'd lost your mum and dad. I don't have any really special friends myself, so if you need one, I'm available. There's no catch. I hope you don't mind freckles or red hair or the odd podgy bit? They've never bothered me. In fact, I've always thought of them as rather attractive. Who looks after you if you don't have a mum and dad any more? Was that old lady your granny?'

We had all seen the slow old lady who had brought Meredith to school. Although, maybe looking back now, she hadn't exactly *brought* her. In some ways, it was more the other way round. Meredith didn't act as though her granny was looking after her, it was more as if she was taking care of her granny, as if she was the one in charge.

When I mentioned Meredith's granny to her, an odd look came over her face. A rather nasty, almost malicious, even triumphant sort of look, as though she didn't really like her granny at all, or as though

13

Meredith were gloating over her for some reason, as though she'd tricked her out of her share of some sweeties or something like that. Straight away, I thought that I must have imagined it, or seen it wrong, or misunderstood. Because Meredith's granny looked like such a sweet old lady when you saw her out in the playground in the afternoon, patiently waiting, with all the other mums and dads, for Meredith to finish school and to walk her home.

'Yes,' Meredith said, 'that's my granny you saw.' Only she said it the way you might say, 'Yes, that's my dustbin, you saw,' or, 'Yes, that's my wart.' She didn't say it with any sense of pride or warmth, or with any note of affection at all. She said it just as if her granny were something nasty she had stepped in and couldn't quite get off her shoes.

Huh, I thought, you don't know how lucky you are having a granny – even if you are unlucky not having a mum or dad. She would have done for a granny for me, and I thought that if Meredith didn't want to be my particular friend, and if she didn't much want her granny either, then maybe I could have her. But on second thoughts I realized that this was pretty selfish, because I already had a mum and a dad, (even if I didn't have a sister) and to go pinching orphans' grannies when they had no one else to look after them in the whole world wouldn't be a very good thing at all.

'Yes,' Meredith went on, a faraway look in her eye, as though she were thinking back to happier days before she was an orphan, 'my granny looks after me now.'

'What's her name?' I asked, as I'm interested in

14

that sort of thing. I'm always keen on finding out names.

'Her name?' Meredith said. 'It's Grace.'

'Grace?' I said. 'You mean as in *before meals*?'

She gave me a blank look. I get a lot of those.

'Grace?' she said. '*Before meals? What do you mean?*'

'Our neighbours,' I explained, 'are very religious and they always say grace before meals. You know, like – "*Thank thee o lord for these thy gifts—*"'

'That's a different sort of grace,' Meredith said coldly. I got the feeling that she didn't like jokes very much – not my jokes, anyway.

'So why did you move to this school,' I asked, changing the subject. 'Didn't you like the old one? Or did they chuck you out?'

'Of course not,' Meredith said, as if offended by the very idea. But I was only asking. I didn't mean anything by it. And besides, just because you've been chucked out of school, it doesn't mean you're a bad person.

'We moved,' she went on, 'to get away from everything.'

'Like what?' I said. 'Couldn't you pay the milkman?'

Meredith paused and looked sad.

'We moved to get away – from the memories,' she said. And she took out a tissue then – and it looked like quite a clean one – and she sort of applied it to her eyes to soak up the moisture, but from where I was standing I didn't actually see any tears coming out at all.

'What memories?' I asked.

'Memories of – of Mum and Dad,' Meredith said,

and she gave her nose a good loud blow, and then sniffed a little and dabbed at her eyes again.

'Oh,' I said. 'I'm sorry.'

I was too, because I don't like to see people upset any more than anyone does. But then, when I thought things over, I was puzzled as well, because if I lost my mum and dad, I wouldn't want to move away from where all the memories were. I'd want to stay there for ever. I'd want to live in Memory Lane itself and I'd walk up and down it every day, thinking back to how things used to be before the tragedy happened.

But maybe it was different for Meredith and her gran. Maybe thoughts of happier times were too much for them to bear, and they just had to get away and start anew, or stay sad and unhappy for ever.

So I didn't blame them really for wanting to get away if that was the case.

But, just the same, I did wonder why Meredith wasn't more affectionate towards her gran. After all, by the sound of it, her gran was the only living relative she had left. But maybe something like that can cause as much resentment as anything else. Maybe if you only have one person left, you start to blame them for the fact that everyone else has gone, and don't like having to rely on them all the time and having no one else to go to. (In which case Meredith would need a special friend more than ever.) Or maybe it was just that Meredith was so young and quick, and her granny was so old and slow, and that made them like oil and water, and chalk and cheese, and Jack and Mrs Sprat, with the fat and lean bits.

Sometimes very old people just don't seem to realize how urgent it all is. They seem to have forgotten and only want to take their time. It's weird really that the less time you have left, the slower you go; and the more time you have, the quicker you take it. You'd think by rights that it would be the other way round.

The bell went for the end of break-time then, and I still hadn't really got an answer to my question. So I asked it again.

'So what do you think then, Meredith?' I said. 'Special friends or not?'

She closed her book, after first dog-earring the corner of the page so that she wouldn't forget her place.

'It's very kind of you, Carly,' she said, 'and while I would very much like to be friends with everyone, as it makes life so much simpler, I'm not really looking for a special friend as such. To be honest, I just wish the day was over. And that tomorrow was over as well. And next week, and the week after that. In fact, all I really want is to be grown up – don't you? Don't you feel that this is all just so—' and she gestured around at the people playing, at the hopscotch grid on the ground, at the climbing frames, at the number snake, at the wooden wigwam for the infants to play in, '—all just so immensely *childish*.'

And before I could reply, she had walked off back towards the classroom, so as to get the next lesson over with as quickly as possible.

Childish! *Childish?* Well, of course it was childish. If children can't be childish, who can? That was the point of being a child, wasn't it; to do what you liked, to muck around, to take your time to grow up, to learn, explore, investigate.

But Meredith – she seemed to have done it all already. That was it, that was how she was different. She had the air of someone who'd 'been there, done that and bought the T-shirt.'

How strange, I thought, how very strange, as I watched her cross the playground, a lanky, disdainful figure, looking down on everyone around her.

'You have to make allowances,' I thought. 'She doesn't mean it. She's lost her mum and dad and only has her granny. Things like that can affect people and make them seem rude when they're not. They're just like woodlice under attack, and they've grown an armour-plated skin and rolled themselves up into little balls so that nobody can get at them. But let them feel safe and secure again, and they'll maybe open up.'

So I hadn't given up on Meredith entirely. It was early days yet. I'd give her a chance to settle in and then maybe ask again in a week or two. She might feel more like having a special friend then, and it was quite possible that I'd still be available.

3

Private Matters

That afternoon the parents, and if not them, then the meeters and greeters, gathered in the playground from three o'clock onwards – even though we didn't finish till quarter past.

I think they got there early for their own sakes, not for ours, just to have a chat and a gossip with each other and to complain about the teachers. If it wasn't that, it would be what my mum called 'private matters'. She was always talking to other parents about 'private matters'. She was supposed to be there to take me home, but quite often I'd be hanging around for ages, waiting for her to finish chatting.

Some afternoons we wouldn't get away until four o'clock, and if I asked what they'd been talking about she'd say not to be nosy. But, of course, if your mum ever asked *you* a question and you said, 'I'm sorry, but I am unable to reveal that sort of information, my dear parent, as it is private matters,' she'd probably have fifty fits.

Grown-ups like to know all your business, that's how it seems to me. And if you're not grown up yet, your duty is not to tell them anything unless you really want to, and even then it's probably a good idea to miss out the gory bits.

Well, a week or so after Meredith began at school, I was out in the playground one afternoon, waiting for my mum to finish another of her long conversations, when I spotted Meredith's granny, Grace, shuffle into the playground and sit on the low wall by the gate to wait for her granddaughter to appear.

Normally she didn't have to wait long, as Meredith was usually very anxious to get away from school and go home, or go to the shops. We had seen Meredith in the shops quite a few times, my mum and I. But she was never looking at toys, only at grown-up things, like clothes and jewellery and expensive perfumes, while her long-suffering granny stood in the background, waiting for Meredith to be ready to move on.

'Oh look at *that*, Gran,' Meredith would say. 'Look at that *fabric*! Look at that *style*!'

But it was all far too old for her, and not meant for girls of her age at all.

Meredith's granny cut a lonely figure in the playground that day. The other grown-ups were always polite to her, and nodded and said hello and asked after her health, but nobody seemed to want to talk to her for long. Maybe she was too old and distant for them, and her concerns weren't their concerns. Or maybe the truth was that she frightened them. I think that sometimes very old folk do frighten people. It's because they remind people of what lies ahead, that we will all be old and frail ourselves one day – at least if we don't die first. But who wants to be reminded of things like that? It's like a blast of cold air on a summer's day, or like a cloud crossing the sun.

To be fair though, even if people had wanted to start up a conversation with Meredith's granny, they rarely got the chance. Because as soon as anyone did start talking to her, Meredith would come tearing across the playground, waving her books and saying, 'I'm here, Gran! Time to go!'

Her gran never dared to say, 'Just a moment, Meredith,' or, 'In a minute dear, run away and play, Granny's talking to someone just now.'

No. She would immediately apologize and excuse herself and break off her conversation in order to take Meredith home or do whatever else she wanted. It was almost as if Meredith was in charge, that she, not her granny, were the adult, the one responsible for all the decisions.

I had noticed something else about Meredith's granny too. It was the way she looked at the children.

I think that Meredith had instructed her granny not to arrive at the school too early – certainly not before ten past three. In fact I overheard Meredith give her a ticking off one day, when she had got to the school early, and we had all seen her chatting to my mum out in the playground. Meredith had hurried out after the bell went, and I heard her say, 'You got here far too early! I told you not to do that! Don't ever let me see you do that again – or there'll be trouble.'

'I'm sorry, Meredith,' her granny had meekly answered, 'I must have misjudged the time. It won't happen again, I'll see to that. I promise.'

After that she never got there until ten past three at the earliest. Though sometimes I would see the tip of her white-haired head visible over the wall, as she waited out in the street, afraid to come into the playground just yet, as it was still too soon, and she would only get into trouble with Meredith.

During those few minutes that she was occasionally alone in the playground though, I saw Meredith's granny watch the children as they streamed out of their classrooms. She watched almost spellbound as they ran and played, shrieking at the tops of their voices. She watched with a kind of hunger and sadness.

It wasn't ordinary watching. Grannies usually watched in a different way. They watched children playing with faraway smiles on their faces, with misty memories of long ago. Rose-coloured-spectacle memories, I mean. They were probably thinking of when they had been girls, of how they had played the same games, or of how things had changed, one or the other or even both. They maybe thought of how *they* had once had grannies too, but now they *were* grannies, and how strange and sad and mysterious it was that they should have turned from small girls to old grannies, and it had all happened so quickly. It was a bitter-sweet watching, that kind of watching. Happy and sad both together.

But Meredith's granny watched the children playing with a dreadful, terrible longing in her eyes. It wasn't like she was remembering the past or growing nostalgic with a warm inner glow. It was as if she wanted to *be* there – up on the climbing frame, there on the grass doing handstands, here with the other girls, turning the skipping rope, or clapping her hands in the clapping game.

It was painful to watch her. There seemed to be so much hurt and longing in her old, sad eyes. It turned a knife in your heart to see her stare so at the children playing around her. Sometimes she would reach out, as if to take the hand of someone running by, as if by doing so she could be young again and join in their game.

Her hand would tremble and her lips would purse a little then, as if she might start to cry. Her hand was so thin too, almost like the claw of a bird, and her arm was stringy and scrawny, like the leg of a chicken. And I know it wasn't her fault, and that we all grow old and it can't be helped. But in some ways it sent the shivers down your spine. It really did. It made you think of terrible things, of things lurking in cellars, of things in wardrobes, of things in attics, of things all covered in cobwebs, and of dungeons where no one dare go.

But more than anything it made you sad, to see the poor old lady seeming to reach out for her lost and faraway childhood, as if she wanted it back.

It was almost as if she had never really had a proper childhood at all.

Maybe I was too busy watching her that afternoon to notice that she was watching me. How long she had been looking at me, I couldn't say. She smiled faintly, in the way that grannies do, and I smiled back, to be polite.

Then I remembered that Meredith was going to be late. She had been roped in for the annual school production by Mr Constantine. He said he needed someone tall and willowy for his leading lady and could Meredith sing? She said she couldn't (though if you ask me she could, she was just trying to wriggle out of it – being the leading lady in the school play was just another of those 'boring' things as far as she was concerned). But Mr Constantine said it didn't matter, and that it was more important to be tall and willowy than it was to be able to sing. Which I disagreed with, as a matter of fact, because it ruled out a lot of shortish, chubbyish girls, especially ones with red hair and freckles, who maybe could sing a bit.

But no. Mr Constantine said that he would teach Meredith how to sing. There is no such thing as tone deaf, Mr Constantine said. There is no such thing as a person who cannot – eventually – sing in tune.

Well, if that's what he believes he ought to come round to our house one night and listen to my dad singing in the bath. It's awful. It sounds like somebody strangling a turkey. The only way you could ever get my dad to sound in tune would be to hammer a large cork into his mouth and muffle him up completely.

To be honest, I was a bit miffed that Meredith had got the leading-lady role in the school play when she had only been in the place a couple of weeks. I had been there for years, and Mr Constantine had never once paid any attention to me.

I was always on at him to put on a production of *Annie* – the musical. I don't know if you're familiar with it, but it's all about another orphan, called Annie, who is the star, and who has red hair and a lot of freckles, somewhat like one or two people that I know. I would suggest it to Mr Constantine every couple of weeks or so, by way of a hint, and to let him know that I was interested. But he said that you would need a very talented kind of actress for a part like Annie. And even when I cleared my throat and coughed a bit to draw attention to my own red hair and freckles and my acting abilities, he still didn't seem to catch on. He just went and did this other play instead. But I don't think that people are all that interested in tall and willowy girls these days. I think they want a change from all that, and would like to see a short, chubbyish person get a chance, instead.

Mr Constantine did offer me a role in the play with Meredith, but it was only a small part as the Third Squirrel. I did feel that I was being under-used and that I could have been the First Squirrel, at the very least. But no. Third Squirrel it was. He promised I would get to wear a costume with a bushy tail, and that the other squirrels and I would also get to sing a song about how we had forgotten where we had hidden our nuts.

I said to Mr Constantine that if we had all forgotten where we had hidden our nuts then we must have been a pretty stupid bunch of squirrels. But he just said, 'Maybe so, Carly'. And then he went on to add that quite often real squirrels *do* forget where their nuts are buried, and so if nothing else, it was true to life. I think he'd read a book about them, or maybe he kept one as a pet.

Anyway, we squirrels didn't have much to rehearse and so we weren't needed for weeks yet. But Meredith had been roped in straight away and had to do a bit after school every Wednesday.

I thought that perhaps Meredith's granny didn't know this, or maybe she had forgotten. Because why else would she have come so early when Meredith wouldn't be out for ages yet? So I went over to tell her, just in case she didn't know, and to explain what Meredith was up to.

'Excuse me,' I said, 'but are you Meredith's granny?'

She gave me a smile. It was a nice old smile, as old smiles go. There were all sorts of wrinkles and crinkles and crows' feet in it. It's amazing where you can get wrinkles if you live long enough.

'Meredith's granny?' she repeated, almost as if a little bit unsure. Then she nodded. 'Yes,' she said. 'I suppose you could say that. That's who I seem to be anyway. Yes. That's who I seem to be now.'

I felt worried then, and wondered if maybe she had gone a bit strange in the head like some very old people do. Mum said that my gran went a bit strange when she got very old, and would walk down to the shops in her dressing gown and try to buy chips in the hairdresser's.

But then Meredith's granny smiled, as if her head had suddenly cleared and things had come into focus.

'You're Carly, aren't you?' she said. 'Meredith's talked about you.'

'That's right,' I nodded. I was a bit surprised that Meredith had mentioned me, I didn't think she'd been that impressed. 'I asked Meredith if she wanted to be my special friend,' I explained, 'as there's a vacancy for one at the moment – but she very politely declined.'

'Yes,' her granny said. 'Meredith isn't the sort of girl who really wants friends. She neither wants nor needs them, I think. That's just how it is.'

26

'Yes,' I agreed. 'Meredith is always very pleasant to everyone, but she does seem a bit, well – faraway.'

The old lady's eyes lit up.

'Yes,' she said. 'You're right. Faraway. Only—'

'Only what?' I said.

'Only I ought – well – to warn you,' she went on.

'About what?'

'Meredith.'

'Meredith? What about her?'

'She maybe isn't . . . quite as nice or as harmless as she seems.'

'Oh?'

I stared at her, shocked. Grannies don't usually come out with things like that, not about their own granddaughters.

'But I can't say any more,' she whispered. 'I daren't. She'll be out any second. And if she sees me talking to you she'll get angry—'

'Why should she get angry? Just for us talking?'

'No, you don't understand. Why should you? And even if you knew, how or why could you ever believe—'

'Believe *what*? Understand *what*?!'

I was getting quite exasperated. I hate it when there are secrets. Especially when I'm not in on them.

'No, please. You'd best go off and play with one of your friends, before Meredith comes out and catches us talking. She'll get angry, she will. And when she gets angry there's always a price to pay, and it's usually me who has to pay it. Quick, go now. Don't get me into trouble. Or yourself. You just can't imagine what she's capable of. You can't imagine what she's done to me – what she's stolen.'

27

And the old lady got more and more upset and flustered until I thought that she was going to faint, or cry, or that her teeth might fall out.

'It's all right,' I said, doing my best to reassure her and calm her down. 'Don't worry, Meredith will be ages yet. That's what I came over to tell you. Maybe she forgot to mention it, but she'll be late out today. She's rehearsing the school play. She's got the tall, willowy part, the one you have to be good-looking for.'

'Oh,' Meredith's granny said, sounding greatly relieved. Then she added, 'In that case—' and she looked around the playground as if to make sure that we weren't being overheard. '—In that case, I wonder if I – if I could confide in you. That is, if you have a moment. You seem like such a kind girl, Carly, so good and kind and patient and understanding. If I told you something would you listen? Would you try to believe me, no matter how strange and incredible my story seemed—?'

'Well,' I hesitated, 'I'll try. I'm not saying I'll swallow anything though. I'll only believe a thing if it really is true.'

'Oh, it is. It really is.'

I looked over to where my mum was sitting on a bench, with three or four other mothers. The matters couldn't have been all that private that afternoon; it seemed as if anyone could join in. She looked as if she'd be ages yet.

'Do you have to get home?' Meredith's granny asked. 'If you do—'

'No. Not yet. I should be all right for half an hour or so.'

'Then let's go and sit over there on the wall, in the shadow of the tree, where it's cool and quiet.'

So we did.

'Oh Carly,' she said. 'It's so wonderful to be able to talk to someone. We'll have to be quick, but first, I just wanted to say how awful it is to have things all bottled up, and not be able to tell anyone. It makes you feel so alone and so hopeless.'

'That's all right,' I said. 'You carry on.'

She looked at me, as if wondering how to start. Then she made a determined face, as though she had decided there was only one way to do it – to jump in with both feet at the deep end.

'OK,' she said. 'OK, Carly, now the first thing you have to know is that although I look like an old, old woman, so old as to be not all that many years away from death itself – well that's only how I *seem*. It isn't how I *am*. The truth is that I'm a young girl. The truth is, Carly, that I'm no older than you.'

4

The Flight

Well, I'd heard of people getting knocked down with feathers before, but I never thought it could happen to me. But if you'd had a feather just then, and given me a poke with it, over I would have gone.

I felt very unsteady as I sat there on the wall, staring goggle-eyed at Meredith's granny, trying to take in what she had just said.

No older than me? But she was *ancient*. She was probably older than Stonehenge, older than the Pyramids, older than that old lawn mower we had in the shed.

A thousand questions came into my mind. I started to ask one of them, but all that came out was a sort of gurgling noise, like when the last of the water goes down the bath plug and it half sucks the sponge down with it.

But Meredith's granny just held her hand up, as though to beg me not to interrupt. So I didn't, as I knew that she was most likely right. If I started asking questions before she'd even started her story, the chances were that she'd never get to finish it. So I managed to stay quiet and let her continue, uninterrupted, and this is what she said:

'Now, I know it's very hard to believe what I just told you,' she continued, 'but it's true just the same – the way a whole lot of impossible sounding things are. I know I look like an old lady, as old as the hills and the valleys too. But the truth is that I'm not old at all. Not inside. Not where it matters. Inside me here, I'm just a girl, the same age as you, Carly, and I shouldn't be trapped in this old body at all.

It's witchcraft and wickedness which have put me here, and evil in its nastiest form – which is evil that doesn't look like evil, but evil masquerading as good.

Now, first of all, my name isn't Grace. And Meredith isn't my granddaughter. The truth is that *I'm* Meredith, and although I can't really prove it to you – or to anyone – I hope that you'll believe me, and maybe try to help me in some way. My body and my youth and my whole life have been stolen from me, you see, Carly, and I'm so sad and unhappy and lonely that I don't know what to do, except to cry. But what good does crying do? It doesn't fix anything.'

I made myself a bit more comfortable on the wall and kept listening.

'I know that Meredith has probably spoken to you and the other children,' the old lady went on, 'and has told you some story about how she is an orphan. Well, the thing about Meredith is that she can be very sly, and clever and convincing too. She can jumble the truth up with all kinds of lies and then shake them up together so that you can no longer tell them apart. Because that's what witches try to do, to confuse and bamboozle you and to leave you bewildered. And that's all she is inside – a witch. She's stolen my body and I'm trapped in hers. She's probably done it before too, and no doubt she'll do it again one day, if she can. That way she'll be able to live for ever, but only at somebody else's expense – the poor, innocent, vulnerable children, whose lives she will have stolen.'

'Wow!' I said. 'Meredith's a witch?' Then I remembered that I wasn't to interrupt, so I just said, 'Wow!' once more and then, 'Go on.'

So she did.

'Now some of what Meredith says is true, and some of it isn't. Some of the things that she says happened to her actually happened to me. So it's not just my body she's stolen, it's my story too. And that's an equally bad and terrible thing when someone steals your story, because it's almost as if they become you, who you were, and what you did.

Now, just forget about the way I look for a while, forget about my wrinkles and my white hair, and think of me as Meredith, the tall, willowy girl – and oh, I did so love to be tall and willowy . . . wouldn't you?'

'Yes,' I nodded. 'I would. As you can see I'm more on the freckly and podgy side. I bet you could be a model if you were tall and willowy like that.'

'Yes,' the old lady nodded, and maybe a tear came to her eye, or maybe it was just that her eyes had got old and rheumy and were watering, the way old eyes do. She paused for a moment to take out her handkerchief. With horror, I noticed something that I hadn't seen before – she had hair on her chin. There wasn't a lot of it. It wasn't like Father Christmas hair, not a great big, bushy beard. But it was hair just the same. I shuddered

32

a little, as though a ghost had walked past me, leaving the fridge door open as it had gone. To have the mind of a girl, I thought, and the body of an old, old lady, with hair on your chin.

It didn't sound nice at all.

The old lady put her hankie back in the pocket of her coat. She seemed faraway then, with a distant look in her eyes. But then she remembered where she was and resumed her story.

'Tall and willowy, that was me. Happy too. With my whole life ahead of me. I was good at all sorts of things, and had lots of friends and not a single enemy at all. I lived in a big house with trees in the garden and two cars in the drive and a grand piano in the front room, which I was learning how to play. We had a gardener in to do the garden and a cleaning lady on Thursdays. Yes, we were almost posh in those days. Not that I thought so at the time, or even realized. It's only afterwards, looking back, that you can see how happy and how fortunate you were.

There was only me in the family, an only child – though Mum and Dad hoped that one day a brother or a sister for me might come along—'

'Same here!' I said excitedly. 'Same here! Except, that is, I used to have a sist—' Then I realized I was interrupting again and bit my lip.

'Those days were wonderful. I went to a really nice school and there was always something to do at the weekends. There was pony riding or dancing classes or gym or swimming or trips away – oh, everything really. And even though I was an only child, that didn't mean I was selfish or spoilt or only interested in myself—'

'Me neither,' I said. Then I remembered I was supposed to be keeping quiet again.

'—No, not at all. We always used to remember those who were worse off than us and we'd do what we could to help them, especially at Christmas and at times like that.

But you know, for all that life was as perfect as life can be, underneath it all I would sometimes get this sense of foreboding, a feeling of unease. And sometimes my dad would look out of the window at our big garden and our cars in the drive and he would say, "Meredith, you should never take anything in this world for granted. Never depend on things remaining as they are for ever. Anything and everything can change. When I was your age, we were poor and had nothing. It was four to a room and two to a bed and not enough to eat a lot of the time. And look at us now – how things have changed for the better. But who knows what might happen tomorrow? Good fortune can change like the tide. All we can do is to hope for the best, and to enjoy what we can of the here and now. Not live *for* the moment, but *in* the moment. The present is all we can be sure of."

So maybe him saying things like that had left me uneasy, with a feeling that everything I depended on could suddenly be taken away. Or maybe I would have worried anyway, because that was my character. But to be honest, most of the time I didn't worry about anything. I was too busy enjoying myself and being happy.

But then the tragedy happened. I was away on a trip with the school and Mum and Dad had gone off for a few days' sailing – because we had a yacht too, in those days, you see. Not a massive yacht, but big enough to sail across to France on. But the yacht was caught in a ferocious storm and it lost its rudder and it hit some rocks, and by the time the lifeboat got to it, it was already too late, for Mum and Dad had both gone, both drowned in the savage sea.'

The old lady stopped speaking and looked down at her hands. Her skin seemed paper thin. You could see the veins underneath. The joints of her fingers were knobbly and swollen, probably with arthritis. She paused for so long that I didn't think she was going to start again. But then, with a kind of sudden determination, as though dragging herself back to reality from the depths of a dream, she picked up where she had left off.

'Well, that was when the nightmare began,' she said. 'It turned out that there were problems with Dad's business and he had used the house as security to raise money for it. It was only a temporary thing, and in another few months we would have been all right. But as it was, the house had to be sold to pay off the firm's debts. So not only was I suddenly an orphan, I was a poor one as well. There was no more private school, no more ponies, no more grand piano, no more dancing lessons. No more anything at all.

At first I went to live with distant relatives, but it didn't work out, as they had problems of their own, and I only seemed to add to them, and eventually I was taken into care. I hated it. It wasn't that the place was nasty or that the people were cruel. It wasn't that. For the most part they were kind and did their best to make you feel wanted. But you didn't feel wanted. You didn't feel wanted at all.

The worst part of it was the beauty parade. That wasn't what it was called, but that was what it amounted to. It was when the people in charge would try to find a home for you – a good home. I always used to think it odd that they would want to find a "good" home for you. As if anyone in their right mind would want to go to a bad one.

"We won't have any trouble finding a good home for *you*, Meredith," the lady in charge of the Care Home used to say. "You're so clean and pretty and have such nice teeth. You shouldn't be a problem at all."

But I was.

When they said I "shouldn't be a problem" what they meant was that I should be fairly easy to get rid of. It gave me the creeps. What they meant, of course, was that as long as you looked nice somebody would give you a home. But I didn't want that sort of home, where all that mattered was whether you fitted in with the furniture and didn't clash with the curtains and you matched the carpets. I wanted a home where someone would care about *me* – the real me, the person inside. I wanted a home where they would still love me even if I looked like a warthog. I wanted someone to love me for me.

So I became what is known as "difficult" and I began to have "a bit of an attitude". And when people came along, interested in fostering or adopting somebody and giving them a home, if I ever heard them use the words "pretty" or "nice teeth", then that was it, I'd have nothing more to do with them, because it was plain to me that they didn't care about me at all, just the way I looked. I was no more to them than a fashion accessory, or a piece of furniture.'

The old lady stopped to get her breath. She plainly hadn't done so much talking in ages, and the effort was tiring her out. I did wonder, though, about all this 'being pretty' stuff. I'm not saying life is easy for tall and willowy people with nice teeth, far from it. But you have to get things into proportion. And if you think 'tall and willowy' is bad, you ought to try 'short, red-haired, covered in freckles and with podgy bits'. That would soon put things into perspective for you.

The old lady moistened her lips. I noticed that even her lips were wrinkled with age. How strange, I thought. Old age was like dust and cobwebs, it could get in everywhere. The old lady's throat was a mass of wrinkles too, like the neck of an ancient turtle.

She picked up the threads of her story.

'Well, there I was, Carly,' she said. 'Alone in the world and with nobody to call my own. The only people who seemed to want me were people who needed a tall, willowy girl to match the new lampstand they had just bought. I almost gave up then. Nobody could get through to me. I ate and slept and went to school and did my homework. But it was almost as if somebody else were living my life for me, and all I did was to watch them. That was me, a watcher. I watched this tall, willowy girl live her life, but I didn't really know who she was any more, except I knew that somehow she answered to my name and that people thought she was me.

So that was how things went on, and they might

have stayed that way for ever. But then Grace arrived.'

'Grace?' I said.

'Yes,' the old lady smiled. '*Me*! Or rather, this body I'm in.' I stared at her. 'Yes. This one,' she nodded. 'This very one here in front of you – Grace. Such a good name, too, don't you think? Grace? You'd never suspect for a moment that it was the name of a witch.'

'But—' I said, remembering my promise not to interrupt or ask questions but interrupting anyway. 'But *how*? I mean, *why*? That is . . . how did . . . how could . . .'

'I'll explain,' she said, 'I'll explain, Carly. Just be patient a little longer.'

So I put my arms around my knees and hugged them tightly, and tried to be patient, but it was difficult.

'When Grace first arrived, I could hardly believe how nice she was. She – that is – this old woman you see in front of you now, she had such a lovely way with her, such a kind smile – you see?'

And she smiled, as if to give a demonstration. It was amazing. The elderly face lit up. The old lady looked like your favourite granny, the one you always wanted but never had – or maybe you *do* have. Then as quickly as she had turned the smile on, she turned it off, and she looked old, cold and unhappy again.

'You see?' she said. 'That was how easy it was for her. You think a smile is a warm and genuine thing. But some people can turn a smile on and off like a tap. They just use it to get what they want, to fool you. They use a smile the way an angler uses bait – to lure the fish on to the hook. Then they pull the line taut and yank you out of the water. And you're caught. But at first I thought Grace was wonderful. It was said that she was quite a wealthy old lady, who had been a spinster all her life—'

'What's a spinster?' I asked. (I reckoned that asking for explanations of words didn't count as interrupting.)

'Well,' Grace said, 'it used to mean a woman who had never married or had children. But lots of ladies don't get married these days, though they still have children, so it isn't quite the same any more. I guess that what people meant by saying that this particular old lady was a spinster was that she didn't have any family of her own. She seemed to be all alone, though I'd heard that she did have a sister somewhere – another elderly spinster, like herself.

Now, because she was wealthy and seemed to want to help children, everyone at the Care Home was very nice to her and she was very nice right back. Perhaps they all had an eye on her money and hoped that she might leave it all to needy children when she died. But dying was the last thing on her mind. Dying was the last thing she intended to do. She was going to make every effort not to die, even if it killed her.

Every week or so, Grace would turn up at the Care Home with presents to hand out to children who had birthdays, or maybe to take them off on a treat – with permission, of course. But if you ask me she wasn't there for the birthdays at all. She was just there sizing people up until she could find the victim she wanted, and it turned out to be me.

On her first visit, the old lady virtually ignored me,

except to ask my name as she was leaving, and to give me a big smile. On her next visit she brought me a present, and though I explained that it wasn't my birthday, she said I was to keep it anyway. On her third visit, she asked the Matron of the Care Home if she could take me and three other children out for a treat. She was given the necessary permission and off we all went in a taxi, first to see a film and then to go for pizza and ice cream. It reminded me of the old days, when my mother and father were still alive.

After that Grace always came to see me when she arrived for a visit. We got friendlier and friendlier, and I soon believed that she was the kindest, nicest old lady I had ever met. And when she asked if I could be allowed to come and live with her, I thought that I could really begin to be happy again, and that I could start to get over the past.

But it wasn't that easy. The Care Home was very strict and there were pages of regulations about who could become a foster parent or a guardian, or who would be allowed to adopt children as their own.

At first it seemed that it wouldn't be possible for me to go and live with Grace. She was too old; she was too frail; she was all on her own; she wouldn't be able to look after me properly, and what would she do in an emergency? But little by little she found answers to all the questions, solutions to the problems and ways to remove every obstacle.

She would get people in to help, she said; she would employ a housekeeper; she would take on a chauffeur to drive a car, so that I could be taken wherever I needed to go. Maybe her sister would be able to help her out from time to time. She would see to it that I had lots of young people around me and arrange for me to have friends over to tea. She would arrange for me to go to a wonderful school, and I would never want for anything or be lonely again. The future all sounded so grand for me – a tall and willowy future to fit me like a glove.

I thought.

One by one she overcame every objection, until at last she was allowed to take me home, as my foster parent and guardian. She just seemed to charm everyone, to have the power to move all obstacles aside, almost as if . . . by magic. One moment people would be saying, "Oh no, you can't possibly look after a girl like Meredith, not at your age." And the next moment, all the lumps and difficulties would have been flattened out and smoothed over. And it was, "Yes, Grace, of course, Grace. I'm sure that won't be any trouble. I'm sure that will be all right. No problem at all."

And their eyes would glaze over, as if they had been hypnotized. And then, of course, she had money, which can lubricate the stiffest joints and oil the creakiest wheels.

I remember the night I packed my bag and got ready to leave the next morning. I was sad to leave some of the friends I had made at the Care Home, but I wasn't sorry to be going. I think that some of the other children even envied me my good luck and good fortune. If only they had known. If only *I* had known, I wouldn't have been so eager to pack my bag. I bet that as I left the Care Home the next morning many of the other children must have

41

watched me go and must have wished to themselves, "If only it was *me* instead of Meredith!"

If only it had been. Now if you'll excuse me a moment, it's time for my pills.'

The old woman reached into the pocket of her drab, frumpy coat and took out a container of tablets.

'Please could you take the top off, Carly?' she asked. 'My hands are too stiff sometimes and my fingers don't work properly.'

I prised the top off the container. (The label said it was child-proof but it wasn't, at least not against children like me.) She shook two red-and-white capsules out into her hand.

'I need them for the inflammation,' she said. 'My joints.'

She swallowed two of the pills, and then took out another container for me to open.

'These too, please,' she said. 'For my poor old heart.'

So I opened that one, and she took another two pills.

'Don't you need water to swallow them with?' I asked.

'It's all right,' she said. 'I'm used to it.' She returned the pillboxes to her pocket. 'Now where was I?'

'You'd moved in,' I said. 'To Grace's house.'

'Ah yes, that's right. So I had. A very nice house it was, too. And everything was just as she had promised. At least it was to begin with. But then things started to change. It seemed that maybe Grace wasn't quite as well-off as she had pretended, and some of her promises didn't materialize. But I didn't

42

mind. I didn't care if there weren't treats and presents all the time, the only thing I really wanted was someone to love me, and a home.

So at first everything was fine, and I had no suspicions that anything wicked was going on at all. Then one evening, three or four weeks after I had moved in, I was sitting in my room just finishing my homework when there was a tap at the door, and Grace came in. She said something strange to me, strange and rather odd and baffling. She said, "Meredith, dear, have you done all your homework?"

"Yes," I smiled, "all done. Would you like to see it?"

"In a moment, dear, yes, though I'm sure it's fine. But first, I wondered if you'd like to go out for a while?"

I looked towards the window. It was dark outside and probably cold. Winter was already settling on the countryside like a blanket – only a blanket to keep you cold instead of warm. And the time was getting on, too. It was late and would soon be bedtime. Where was there to go?

"Out, Grace?" I asked. (Grace was what she had asked me to call her.) "Out where?" She smiled her usual warm, kindly smile.

"How about doing some flying?" she said.

I thought for a moment that she had gone mad. Then I thought that I had misheard. Or maybe I had gone mad. Or maybe she had bought an aeroplane, or a helicopter, or a hang glider or . . .

"Flying?" I said. "Where to? Where from?"

Maybe she was proposing that we fly away to

Paris at the weekend to go round the shops and art galleries. But no.

"Flying from *here*, dear," she said. "From right here. We can do it ourselves and we don't need an aeroplane at all. How about we fly round your room? And then, when we've got the hang of that, we can go out."

Well, I put it down to old age. I knew that sometimes when people got to be very old they could go a bit funny, and I thought that must be the explanation. It worried me though, the thought of Grace going funny. Because if she got so funny in the head that she had to be taken into care, then I would have to go back into it, too. Which was the last thing I wanted. So I decided not to act surprised, and to go along with what she was saying, as though her suggestion that we fly around the room was all perfectly normal.

"You lie down on your bed, Meredith dear," Grace said, "while I get comfortable on the chair here, and we'll try to relax, and then I'll show you how to do it. Oh, and in case you're wondering – or worrying – it isn't *physical* flying that I'm talking about, it's more mental flying, more of a spiritual thing. It's called 'astral projection'. Anybody can do it if they put their mind to it. It's just a matter of building up your mental muscles. Rather like a weightlifter in a gym. At first you can't lift up the large weights. But you try and try. You start on the lighter ones and gradually work your way up to the heavier ones. Until finally, you can do it. You can lift the heaviest one there is."

I was still none the wiser. But I went along with it to keep her happy, and I lay down on the bed, my head on the pillow, and tried to relax.

"Right you are, dear," Grace went on. "Now let yourself grow heavy, every limb and joint, and every part of you. Start with your toes and work your way up to the top, until even the hairs on your head seem relaxed. And while you do that, I'll do the same."

I did as she said. I sort of let go of everything, if you can imagine that. In my head I talked to each bit of me as I worked my way up.

"Left little toe," I said, "relax! Next biggest left toe, relax too."

Then when I had finished all the left toes, I moved on to the right toes. Then it was back over to the left ankle, then the right ankle. Then it was legs and knees and chest and arms, elbows, fingers, shoulders, neck, ears, eyes until finally – just as Grace had said – the very hairs on my head seemed relaxed.

I wasn't asleep though. I was still wide awake. But it was as if my body had gone from me, as though I was no longer inside it, as though it no longer really belonged to me, or even mattered.

"Relaxed now?" I heard Grace's voice ask.

"Yes," I heard someone answer. And although the voice was my voice, I didn't remember speaking.

"Good," Grace said. "Then concentrate. Imagine a spot above your head, up on the ceiling. Concentrate on it as hard as you can and think of nothing else. Try to become totally absorbed in this imaginary spot above you. Let it become you, and you become it. Let it fill and completely occupy your mind. Then, when you have done that, tell me what you see."

I did as she instructed. I was curious now. I wanted to find out what would happen. My eyes were closed by then, but I wasn't asleep. I was more in a trance. I pictured the ceiling above me and I imagined a spot upon it, a small red disc, no bigger than a beam of torchlight. I thought of nothing but that imaginary circle. I let it absorb all my thoughts; I let it soak me up into it, as though I were a puddle of water and it was a dry sponge.

I don't know how long I lay like that. It could have been minutes or hours. I neither knew nor cared. Gradually, I lost all awareness of myself, of my own body, of my itchy nose. I began to see something. My eyes were still closed, but I could see something. At first I didn't know what. It was vague and blurred. Then things came into focus. It was as if a mist was clearing. Slowly the picture started to make sense. I was looking down on something, and this is what I saw.

Beneath me was a room, a bedroom. A girl's bedroom from the look of it, decorated in the kind of colours that a girl would choose, and filled with the kind of things that a girl would have. There were sketch pads, clothes, some fluffy toys, a hula hoop, some books, some crayons, some paints, a half-finished friendship bracelet lying on the bedside table.

In one corner of the room was a wicker chair, and in that chair was an elderly lady. Her hands were folded in her lap and she seemed asleep. In fact she barely seemed to be breathing, so still and quiet she was. She could even have died, just slipped quietly away. But then I could see that she was breathing after all. Her chest rose slowly and a soft sigh escaped from her lips.

I looked further around the room. This time I saw a bed, a single bed, directly beneath me. Upon the bed was a girl, a brown-haired, willowy sort of girl. She too appeared to be asleep, and was also almost imperceptibly breathing. Then I looked at the girl's face, and I saw something terrifying and quite unbelievable.

The girl was me.

I was looking down at my own body. Somehow my mind, my spirit, my soul, my very self – call it what you like – was no longer down there inside my earth-bound form. I was here, floating above myself, like a small cloud hovering around the ceiling of my room. I was as light as a feather – lighter – without any weight or real shape or form at all. I could move about too, if I put my mind to it. I could go from one corner of the room to another, change my viewpoint and perspective. One moment I was there above the bed. The next – by a mere act of will – I was over by the window. Then I was by the lampshade. Then I was looking down upon the old lady again. Then—

I heard a voice. Only not with my ears anyway, but more with my mind. I heard it the way you hear voices in dreams, and it was calling my name.

"Meredith," it said. "Is that you? Is everything fine?"

It was Grace's voice. I looked down at her body. It was still inert in the wicker chair.

"I'm OK," I said – or rather I *thought*. But I felt sure that thinking was enough, and wherever she was, she would hear me, just as I was hearing her. Only where was she? As if reading my thoughts her voice answered.

"I'm here too," she said. "In the corner of the room. Just above the table. Your bedside lamp is right underneath. I can look down through the top of the shade and see the bulb."

I looked to where she said she was, but of course I could see nothing. You can see a body, but how can you see a mind?

"I can't see you," I said. "I can see you down in your chair asleep, but I can't see *you*."

"Nor can I see you," her voice told me. "But I know that you're there. So what do you think, Meredith? How does it feel? Do you like to fly?"

Of course I did. Who wouldn't? It was the most wonderful thing that had ever happened to me. I had never imagined that such things were possible. Maybe we all fly sometimes in our dreams, the way we all try to run away sometimes, but we can't get away from what is chasing us, our legs just go into slow motion and whatever is pursuing us is gaining all the time – until we wake up kicking and screaming and yelling for someone to come.

If there is someone to come. Only for some children there is nobody to come. Not when the nightmares really start, as they did for me.

Maybe I should have been on my guard. Perhaps I should have suspected and have asked myself why that old woman had showed me all this. Why had she taught me how to escape from my body? *Why?*

But I believed that she was good. That she was a kind and loving person, who had rescued me from misery and loneliness. All I could think was how lucky I was to have met such a wise old lady, who knew how to do such marvellous things and who was willing to teach them to others.

"Can we go outside, Grace?" I asked. "Like you

48

said? Can we go out flying around the garden and along the street? Over the houses and the fields and roads? Can we fly over the city, and look down on everyone and everything and all there is to see? Can we, can we?"

I seemed to hear faint laughter then. Not unkind, mocking laughter. Just the laughter you get when grown-ups think you are being too enthusiastic and want to do too much at once. When you want to run before you can walk, as they say, or want to bite off more than you can chew.

"I think it's a little late now, dear," I heard Grace's voice say. "Look at the clock."

I did. I looked down at the girl on the bed who was still in her sleep-like trance. I looked at the clock on the table beside her. Two hours had passed. A whole two hours since Grace had first said to me, "Now let yourself grow heavy. Start with your toes . . ."

It was way past my bedtime. I should have been asleep by now. I should have been in my pyjamas, with my teeth brushed and my face washed and my pillow punched into shape the way I like it, and the light out and a glass of water by my bed in case I woke up thirsty in the night. Two hours? It seemed impossible for two hours to have gone by like that so quickly.

"Can't we go outside just for a moment?" I pleaded. "Just for a minute or two?"

"No, another time, dear," Grace's voice said, firm and insisting. "We must get back to our bodies now. Projecting your mind and spirit like this can be extraordinarily tiring. You'll need to sleep now, or you'll be exhausted in the morning."

I looked down at my body, immobile on the bed.

"But I *am* asleep," I said. "More or less. I'm certainly not doing anything strenuous."

"Oh, but you are, Meredith," Grace said. "You may not seem to be, but you are. Come now. Let's go back."

"Can we do it again, then?" I asked. (I was almost prepared to threaten that if we couldn't do it again I wouldn't go back. How little I knew then. How little.)

"Of course."

"Soon?"

"If you like."

"Tomorrow?"

"Well, maybe not tomorrow."

"When then?"

"At the weekend. When it's not a school day the next day, and you don't have to get up so early in the morning."

"Promise?" I said.

There was the laughter again. The soft, gently amused laughter.

"Promise? Of course, dear. If it's what you want."

"And we can go *outside* next time?"

"Wherever you want to, dear. Wherever you say. Now come, let's go back."

Then it hit me. The way it hits you when you realize you've lost your wallet, or forgotten something important. That sudden bolt of fear. That sudden feeling of "Oh, no! What do I do? What do I *do*!"

I didn't know how to get back in.

I didn't know how to get back into my own body.

There it was, lying on the bed, looking so relaxed

and peaceful, and here I was, looking down on it and
– *I didn't know how to get back in*!

To be honest, I don't know why she didn't do it
then. But maybe there were reasons. Maybe she
wasn't yet strong enough herself. Maybe she didn't
know how strong I was. Maybe I was too near to her
and she realized that she might not have enough time,
or that it would be too much of a struggle. So no. She
didn't try that until later. Although she could perhaps
have done it then. I'm sure that she must have
thought of it.

"Grace!" I cried. And if a mind, if a spirit, if a soul
can scream, mine certainly screamed just then.
"Grace! I can't get back in. I don't know how to get
back into my body! I'll be stuck . . . look at me . . .
my body . . . with no spirit or mind . . . I'll never wake
up – I can't get back in!"

That laughter again. Pitter-pattering like summer
rain. Like rain on a warm day. A brief shower of
pleasant, cooling rain. And next there is a rainbow
and blue sky.

"Don't worry, dear," her voice called reassuringly.
"No need to panic. Just imagine yourself back
again."

"Imagine myself?" I said uncertainly. "How,
Grace? What do you mean?"

"Imagine yourself as you were – imagine yourself
back in your body, being yourself. Remember what it
was like. Remember how it felt to have fingers, to
move your legs. Remember the feel of the pillow
under your head, the weight of your watch strap
around your wrist. Remember how it feels to be you.
And in no time—"

51

"*I'm back*!" I yelled. I sat up. Back in my own body, there on my own bed. "I'm back, I'm back. It feels as though I've been away for years. Yet it's only been an hour or two. And here's my body, the same as it ever was and feeling just as nice."

I stood and crossed over to the chair where the shape of the old lady was coming back to life too. Her eyes opened and looked up at me, crinkled in the corners with the marks of age and laughter.

"We're back, Grace," I said. "Thank you, thank you! That was so wonderful. To fly like that. It was amazing. And it's so wonderful to be back too. Isn't it? To come back into your own body, it's – I don't know – so old and familiar and yet so fresh and new! It's wonderful to have a body, isn't it Grace? Don't you think? To be able to breathe and move and see and hear and walk and talk. Isn't it so absolutely wonderful? And don't we just so take it all for granted?"

She looked at me, and her eyes seemed cold, lizard cold, snake cold and ancient as Egypt.

"Oh yes, we do, Meredith," she nodded. "We do so take it all for granted. Especially, in many ways, *young* people. They take their youth so much for granted. Almost as if they will always be young and things will never change. As if they will never grow old."

Then she became her nice, warm, normal self again, and I immediately forgot all about that lizard cold-ness in her eyes. Right then I was just too excited. I helped her up out of the chair. Her poor old bones had grown stiff with sitting so long and she didn't seem able to stand unaided.

"Thank you, Meredith dear," she said. "You're so young and agile, aren't you? So young and supple, and here's me so old and decrepit now, with hardly even the memory of a handstand in my head."

"But you've become such a wonderful old lady, Grace," I said, trying to comfort and console her, as she had been so kind to me. "And you've had such a long and rewarding life, so full of interesting things, I bet. And you've travelled all over the world, haven't you, wasn't that what you said? And you know how to project yourself out of your body and how to fly in the sky – and that's more than most people have ever done. Isn't it?"

"Yes, dear," she said. "You're right, of course. I've had a long and enjoyable life. I can't complain. I've no right to expect any more, have I? I've had my share of youth and pleasure. I musn't grumble. No, I can't complain or expect any more than I'm entitled to."

I didn't really know what to say then, because although there was nothing wrong with the words she said, the tone in which she said them was filled with bitterness. Yet it still didn't occur to me to be suspicious of her, to think that she could be anything other than the kindly old lady she seemed. Or that far from having my welfare at heart she had other plans for my future, that she had deliberately sought me out, a lonely, solitary girl, without friends or close relatives. Someone who – in many ways – nobody would really miss.

The fact was that I didn't believe in witches. Witches were for fairy stories, and fairy stories weren't the kind of things I believed in any more.

53

So even when I asked, "Where did you learn how to do such things, Grace? How to project your mind outside of your body and to look down upon yourself like that?" and when she answered, "Oh, it was just something somebody taught me once, dear. Something known by the select few," even then it never crossed my mind that these things could only be accomplished by mysterious forces of which I knew nothing. Forces such as witchcraft.

Grace went to the kitchen to make herself a warm drink and I got ready for bed. She had been right. I felt exhausted and I fell asleep immediately, even before she came up with my glass of water and my hot water bottle to say goodnight. But I knew she had done. Because when I woke in the morning, the glass of water was there, untouched by my bed, and when I stretched out, my feet touched the hot-water bottle. Only it wasn't hot any more, but not quite cold either, just somewhere in between.

She called me down for breakfast at the usual time. I sat eating my cereal wondering about the night before. Maybe I had dreamt everything, the flying included.

"Grace," I said, "last night – I had this dream . . ."
She smiled.

"Yes," she said. "I thought it was a dream too the first time it happened to me."

"So it wasn't?"
"No."
"It really happened?"
"It really happened."
"I can fly?"
"It certainly seems that way," she laughed.

54

I went to school that morning with the same three words buzzing round in my head. I wanted to shout them out loud to everyone I could see. I wanted to tell my friends, my teachers, everyone on the buses and the trains, in the streets and the traffic jams, the shops and the cafés.

"I can fly!" I wanted to yell. I wanted to tell the whole world. "My spirit has wings! I can fly!"

But who would ever have believed me? Nobody, that's who. They'd have thought I was a crackpot, and put me back into care, or somewhere worse, like an institution for unbalanced girls with serious delusions. So I kept it to myself. But nobody could stop me from thinking. And that was what I thought, over and over, all day long. It went through my head like the refrain from a song that you just can't forget.

I can fly, I can fly, I can fly!'

5

The Trap

'Now, before I go on, Carly, there's just one thing I have to say. There's one thing I have to warn you about. And that is the ways of wickedness. Because wickedness and evil don't always arrive with a frightening snarl and an ugly face. Sometimes those who seem kindest and most friendly are the wickedest of all. Wickedness doesn't lie in how people appear, or even in what they say. Good or evil lies in what people do. It's what we do to each other that counts. Nice words and promises and pretty faces are all well and good, but nothing really matters as much as what is done.

And sometimes, you know, the nicest smiles, the sweetest promises and the prettiest faces can turn out to be the most wicked of all. So be warned, Carly, be warned. Be very, very careful and always be on your guard.

Well, that day after my spirit first left my body and flew around the room, I couldn't concentrate on a single thing but one – on getting home and doing it all over again. Only this time I would travel wider and further and explore all there was to see.

I don't think I took in a single word of a single lesson, and if I wrote any notes down, then my pen must somehow have managed to do so all on its own. Because I know that I wasn't listening to anything the teacher said.

As soon as I got home I called to Grace – who was lying on the sofa in the sun-filled living-room, resting as she did every afternoon, for her age and her arthritis could make her very tired.

"Grace! It's me! I'm home! Can we do it again? Can we? The flying? The astral projection or whatever it's called? Can we do it again? Both of us? Right now? I know you said we'd have to wait until the weekend, until it wasn't a school day, but can't we just have a little fly around? Can't we?"

She just laughed.

"Meredith, Meredith, slow down a little, dear, do. You're like a tornado, the way you burst into the house, opening all the doors and sending everything fluttering. Oh, it's such a tonic to see you, dear. To be so young and so full of life. It gladdens an old woman's heart."

But I wasn't bothered about any of that. I only had one thing on my mind.

"Can we, Grace, can we?" I pestered her. "Or if you don't want to, can I do it on my own?"

Well, of course I didn't really need to ask that. I could have tried to do it on my own without her, or anyone else's permission at all. What was to stop me from simply going up and lying on my bed and letting myself go heavy and then floating away up to the ceiling like before? Maybe even out of the window this time too. And over the gardens. And all the way to outer space.

I was afraid. That was the truth of it. I wanted

Grace to be with me in case something went wrong. I couldn't imagine quite what that would be, but I had a sense of foreboding all the same. I wanted someone to be with me, someone who would know what to do in an emergency.

"Shall we go flying again, Grace? Shall we? Later on then? After tea? You're not too tired, are you? And I'm sure it will do you good. People are always saying that it does you good to get out and I'm sure that's so. Especially to get out of your own body for a while. Don't you think?"

Grace smiled up at me from the sofa. The sun was shining on her and she had to crinkle up her eyes. I saw how paper-thin her skin seemed to be in the afternoon sunshine. It reminded me of old paintings in museums of people who are about to go to heaven in a beam of light.

"Tea and homework first," she said. "And then we'll see."

I used to hate it when people said, "And then we'll see," because that usually turned out to mean "No". It was just a means of fobbing you off. But I felt that on this occasion it would turn out to mean "Yes".

And so it did.

After tea I did my homework. I didn't do a very good homework that night as I hadn't paid much attention to any of the lessons during the day. But I got through it somehow and then went in search of Grace, to remind her about her promise, in case she had forgotten, as old people can become very absent-minded. (So can young people, but in old ones you notice it more. Also a forgetful young person is just forgetful, but a forgetful old one might be losing her marbles.)

She hadn't forgotten though. She was waiting in the living-room, sitting on the sofa again, reading a big, heavy book, the size of a bible. Only it wasn't a bible.

Grace was always reading those big, heavy books. And I do mean big and I do mean heavy. They even had metal clasps on them to shut them tight, and had you wanted to you could have put a small padlock into the clasps to lock the book up so that nobody else could read it.

Grace didn't lock up the books she read, she just kept them in her room. Had she left them lying around I don't think I'd have bothered to read them much. They looked so old and boring. I did open one once and glanced at the title page, but it was all in funny italic writing and so hard to read that I didn't bother after a line or two. All the "s" letters in the words looked like an "f", so that something like "dress" would have appeared as "dreff". I just closed the book anyway, and left it on the table. Grace had come into the room shortly after and taken it away.

"I wouldn't like these books to get damaged, dear," she said. "They're very old and rare and valuable. Collector's items, you might say."

I remember that one of those old books, with its marbled-paper, its brass corners and leather spine, had its title etched upon it in faded gold leaf. It was a word I had come across once before, but whose meaning I couldn't quite recall. The word was "Necromancy".

Anyway, Grace closed her book as I came into the room, and she put it down on the table by the sofa.

"Homework done?" she asked.

"Yes," I said.

"All of it?"

"Yes."

"Every bit?"

She was just teasing me, trying to spin it out until we could get started.

"Now there was something you wanted to do again, wasn't there, dear? Something we'd arranged? Only what was it now? I'm getting so absent-minded."

"Fly, fly, *fly!*" I cried. "You know what it is, Grace. You're only teasing. You do remember, don't you?"

"Yes, of course," she beamed. "Come on. You sit down there in the armchair and I'll stay here on the sofa, and then we can begin."

Which is exactly what we did. And just as before I let myself relax, and I seemed to grow heavier and heavier. I started with my smallest toe and worked my way up to the tips of my ears and to the end of my nose, to my eyebrows and the hair on my head. I told everything to be still, to relax, to grow heavy and quiet, to forget that it even existed.

Next, I concentrated on that imaginary spot above my head, somewhere up on the ceiling. I focused upon that spot the way you bring the rays of the sun together through a magnifying glass into a pinpoint of intense heat, hot enough to set fire to paper and to shrivel up dead leaves—

And then I was flying again, flying around the room. There beneath me, seemingly asleep in an armchair was a girl just like me, my body, the rest of me. But my spirit was flying, as free as a bird, ready to soar higher, and to fly further and further.

I felt like laughing and shouting for joy. Only I had no lungs to laugh with, no breath to shout with. Those things belonged to the girl in the chair. Me, I was laughter itself, and joy itself. I didn't need to express those things. I was them.

"Are you there, dear? Are you free?"

It was Grace's voice, yet not her voice at all. It was like a mind within a mind – hers within mine. I looked down and there was her old, tired body, lying still on the sofa. But her voice sounded younger, as if she was pleased to be liberated for awhile from the burden of her old self.

"Which way?" I asked. "Where do we go?"

"Wherever we want to, Meredith. Come on. Let's start with the garden."

"But how?"

"Just go. Just will yourself to be there. Just follow me."

Follow me. Such a strange thing to say. How could I follow someone I couldn't even see. And yet somehow I could. I had sensed her just ahead of me, floating towards the window. So I floated with her and then—

—I was out. And away.

The garden was beneath me now. I was higher than the willows and taller than the oaks.

"Are you there, Meredith? Are you there?"

"Yes. Yes. I'm over here, flying above the redwoods. I can see the birds and the squirrels and look – there's a cat climbing up into the branches, and down there in the garden, a hedgehog crossing through the grass. It probably thinks that no one can see it. But we can, we can. We know what you're doing!"

"Come on, dear. Let's explore."

I followed the voice within my head – well, within my mind; my head was back in the living-room, lolling on the armchair.

"Come on, Meredith, over here."

We moved on. We left our garden and flew over others. There were children on climbing frames, ladies with watering cans, men with mowers, trimming the lawn. Old car tyres hung from branches. There were tennis courts and croquet lawns and bowling greens in the park.

Soon the houses were fewer and the gardens turned to fields. There were tractors ploughing. In others the farmers were leading the cattle back from milking. There were fields with horses and cantering ponies, fields with sheep grazing, fields with windowless wooden buildings, like barracks or prisoner-of-war camps – they were probably factory farms, full of unhappy turkeys or sad chickens. I felt sorry for them and wished I could do something to set them all free.

Then we were over a road busy with cars, then we were over a motorway, which was jammed solid with unmoving traffic. Then we seemed to be heading for the river estuary, and in the distance I could see the pale yellow of a sandy beach, and the glint of blue water and the white-capped foam of the waves. The sail of a sailing boat filled up like a balloon and the boat gusted away like a piece of driftwood on a racing tide.

"This is wonderful, Grace, isn't it?" my mind called. "Don't you think? Isn't this so wonderful? It's just like magic!"

But there was no reply.

I called again.

"Grace! Grace!"

No answer. No answer anywhere. Not from within me or from around me or—

"Grace! Grace! *Grace!*"

Panic was rising in me now. An awful, terrible fear. I didn't know where I was. Where had Grace gone? What if something had happened to her? What if I couldn't get back? What if I couldn't find my way home?

What if Grace had died? Lying back in the house, on the sofa? What if her heart had given out? And her soul had returned to it?

I was lost. Lost and afraid. The shadow of a rain cloud moved over the sea. The sun was setting on the far horizon, a great bubble of red and gold in a cloud-streaked sky.

I had no body to feel with, and yet I felt terribly cold. In an instant the world had turned from light to dark, from happiness to fear. I was alone and lost and didn't know the way home.

"Grace, Grace, *GRACE!*"

Not even the echo of an echo. Just the cries of the gulls and the running of the waves.

I turned and flew back the way I had come, looking for familiar landmarks, trying to recollect when I had last "seen" Grace, that is when I had last heard her voice in my mind, calling for me to follow.

This way, dear. This way. Left by the church

63

steeple. Right by the barn. Fly straight over the village and then on over the river.

"Grace! Grace!"

Nothing. No one. The landmarks had changed. Things looked different now in the fading light.

I followed the river inland. It was inky black now in the dusk. On I flew. Maybe I had gone too far? But no. There was another river beneath me – a great river of light. The motorway with the grid-locked traffic. The drivers had all put their lights on, as if to guide me home.

Back over the farms and the fields and the gardens; back over the barns and the hedgerows and the steeples. The tennis courts were empty now. The children had left the swings. Lights were on in the bedrooms and bathrooms. Baths were running, kettles were boiling, hot-water bottles were being filled, cocoa was brewing.

It was late, late. It was bedtime. Time to be tucked up. Time to read for a while. Time to ask for a glass of water to delay the inevitable turning off of the light. Time to say goodnight. Time for a hug, a cuddle, a kiss. Time to drift, time to forget, time to dream, time to fly.

I took a wrong turning. I must have done. None of it looked right. Not the roads, the roofs, the houses. And what were all those shops doing there? And that cinema? No. I'd gone wrong.

There was my school. I recognized the sports field and the playground. I could see the markings of the sports pitches, looking white in pale moonlight.

At least the moon was out. That was something. At least I could see my way. I knew where to go now.

Just follow the streets. The way the bus went. Right and left and straight on and no need to stop for the traffic lights.

Just fly. Just fly on.

Then there it was. My prayers were answered. *"Dear God, I'll never be naughty again if only you'll let me find my way home."*

And God had. And I would have to keep my side of the bargain now.

But first to get back.

There was the house, the garden. There was the living-room. Just as we had left it. The curtains open. The lights on.

Down I came. Level with the window, now, and looking in. The big picture window. The one you can slide back in the summer, which leads directly out to the garden.

It was going to be all right. Whatever had happened to Grace, at least I was all right. Oh, I know that sounds selfish, but it was true. It was just how I felt. And I *was* worried for Grace, I *was*. I was worried and concerned, and I wanted to help her. But how could I help without first helping myself? I needed to return to my body, to raise the alarm, to try to find her, to understand what had happened.

I hesitated a moment before flying into the room. I could see Grace asleep – it looked that way, at least – on the sofa, her body just as she had left it. Her chest rose and fell. She was breathing. She wasn't dead. I felt so relieved. At least she was still alive then, at least—

But then I saw something in that room which chilled me to the core of my being. I realized then that you don't need a body to feel fear. Fear is a thing that strikes the centre of your very soul.

I felt as we all must feel sometimes – afraid of the darkness, terrified of the unknown. There's something in the shadows, some creature hiding in the folds of the curtains, some ferocious animal, with ragged claws waiting for us on the other side of the door. But we cannot stay where we are. We have to walk over, draw back the curtains, open the door, and stare horror and terror, and even death in the face.

I looked into the room. There was Grace, still in a trance in the sofa. But when I looked at the armchair, I was no longer there. My body had gone. I was no longer asleep, in a deep hypnotic-like state. I had vanished. I looked around frantically. Where was I? Where had I gone? And then I saw it. My body was there, yes. But it was no longer sitting in the chair, with its eyes closed, its hands folded.

It was dancing. There was no music. But it was dancing.

Dancing like a thing possessed.

Like a thing possessed by someone else's soul . . .

It danced and spun, shrieking and laughing. It jumped over the furniture and screeched with joy, full of the exuberance of being young and alive. It was as full of happiness and as free from care as a newly born lamb, like a creature suddenly young – or suddenly young *again*.

I felt as if in watching this life and vitality, I was looking at my own death. I watched as I did a handstand. A cartwheel. A somersault. A back-flip. (But I couldn't *do* back-flips. When had I learned to do that?) Another cartwheel again. Then I began to laugh. I heard myself laugh. My voice. My laughter. Me, and yet not me. The inflexion was different, my mannerisms had changed.

I cackled. With malice, with pure evil. I walked up to the body of the old woman still in a trance on the sofa. I pointed at her with my forefinger, it was stretched out like a talon, something I never did.

"Who's old *now*?" my voice jeered. "Who's the old ratbag now! Whose turn to be old and slow now, eh, Meredith? Yours, young lady, I think. Maybe that'll teach you to be so stupid and trusting. Maybe it will. Whose turn to use the walking stick and wear the frumpy clothes now, eh, Granny! Yes, yours! You can have the false teeth and the failing eyesight and the hairy chin! It's all yours! It's my little present to you and I hope you enjoy it!"

Then I did a little victory dance, shouting, "Meredith's a granny! Meredith's a granny! That'll teach you! That'll show you! Meredith's a granny!"

My spirit froze. I peered in at myself in the living-room. The body that had once been mine turned and looked out of the picture window. It stared straight at me as though it could see my immortal soul.

"Are you there?" I heard my voice ask. "Have you found your way back yet? Are you there? Watching by the window? Are you? Well, don't stand on ceremony. Come in, young lady, come in. Or is it more '*old lady*' now? It's up to you, of course, but as far as I can see, it's come in or die. It's come in or be a lost soul for ever, a soul without a body. But you can't have *this* body, I'm afraid. This tall, willowy, young one. This one's spoken for. This one's already taken.

It's a very nice body though, isn't it? Don't you think? Let me give you a twirl."

My body spun and pirouetted like a ballet dancer, then stopped to face the window again.

"Good, isn't it? Isn't it just so wonderful to be a girl again, to be young. Not that you'll ever know now! All you're going to be now is *old* – instantly. Isn't that *good* of me? I've saved you all the trouble of having to *grow* old! *You* won't become a teenager and pass exams and get a job and fall in love, or have children of your own and watch them grow up and have children of their own, and all that sort of rubbish. No. You won't have to bother with any of that, you see, because *I'm* going to live *your* life for you! You can have my old body and I can have your new one. Isn't that a good deal? Isn't that just a tremendous bargain? Just like Aladdin, isn't it? New lamps for old. Only it's new bodies for old in this case. And I've got the new one. Lucky me!"

I could only watch. It was as if I had turned to stone, as though I had become a tree in a petrified forest. The girl in the room went on dancing and spinning and jeering. It was still me, but less and less me as each moment went by.

Then it came to me. The meaning of that word. The word in gold lettering on the thick, heavy book: "Necromancy". I remembered now. I had heard it explained during a lesson at school. It must have been buried deep, somewhere in my memory, and now it returned to the surface.

Necromancy meant magic, enchantment or – witchcraft.

Grace was a witch. An old witch. Growing older

68

and soon to die. Unless she could find a younger body, of course, and someone to swap with. Someone to trick and deceive. Someone innocent and vulnerable, trusting and naive. Someone alone in the world and desperate for love and security and a home.

Me.

"Are you out there, Meredith? Your body's waiting, dear. Come in. Put it on. Try it out for size. You might find it a little bit, well, what shall I say – unusual to start with. It's not what you're used to. A bit droopy, not as good a fit. But you will get used to it. I assure you. You don't have much choice. And I'd come in soon, if I were you. The astral projection can't last too long. Did I forget to mention that? Well, the fact is that if you leave a body without a soul for *too* long, it will simply up and, well, die. So be quick, dear. Hurry now. Or there won't be a body for you at all. Not even a second-hand, jumble sale sort of body, like this one."

I entered the living-room. I simply walked through the glass, just by willing it. There was the old lady's body, draped on the sofa like an empty garment. It was as if the finery of my youth had been taken, and all I was left with in exchange was some crumpled old dress.

But the witch was right. I had no choice. I had to wear what there was. There was nothing else. It was that or live as a disembodied, homeless soul for ever. I looked at the body. I shuddered in my mind. Was this really what I had to put on? This old thing? *This.* I pictured myself inside the old woman's body. I imagined it as best I could.

"I'm there now," I thought, "I'm there."

Then suddenly I was.

I screamed.

My eyes opened. I looked around me, but I couldn't see. Terror and horror gripped me again. Slowly, things swam into focus. I had to look through the glasses, of course. Images became sharper.

I saw the face of a grinning, sneering, jeering girl.

"Old bag!" she chortled. "Now who's the old bag!"

I wasn't going to have that. I wouldn't put up with it. Not a moment longer. I raised my hand to give her a good smack. But when I went to raise them, my hand – both my hands – ached with this nagging pain in all the joints of my fingers, and in every knuckle.

The cackling face grinned.

"Hands hurt, do they? It's called arthritis, Granny. Try standing up. You'll find you've got it in your knees too. Not very nice, is it? Quite painful, in fact. I know because I used to have it myself. But I don't any more. It's more of an old person's problem, you see. And me, I'm young, young, *young*!"

And she turned a cartwheel right there before me, just like someone waving a huge bundle of money in front of some starving, homeless person who had no money at all.

"Na, na, nee, na, na!" She wiggled her bottom at me.

"Stupid old granny. Silly old bag!"

Tears came to my eyes.

"Why are you doing this, Grace?" I asked her. "Why? *Why?* What did I ever do to you that you should treat me like this?"

She put her head to one side and looked at me.

70

"What did you ever *do*? You don't get it, do you? *Nothing*. You didn't *do* anything. You were *good*. Get it now? A little goody two-shoes who had lost her mum and dad. *That's* what you did wrong. You fell into my clutches. You were taken in. Fooled rotten and robbed blind! See, you don't have to do *anything* to witches for them to do something to you. Oh, no! That's not how it works at all. We do things like this for the sheer *fun* of it. For the joy of the wickedness! We don't do things to get our own back. We just *do* them!"

"Grace, please, give me my body back, my self, my youth. I want to be a child again. It's not fair—"

"*Fair*!" she screeched. "What's *fair* got to do with it? What about *me*, having to grow old and get arthritis and false teeth and not be able to be young any more. Was that *fair*! Was it?"

"No, maybe not," I said, in the old lady's voice that was now my own. "Maybe it isn't fair that people should have to grow old and die. But that's how it is for everyone. And I should be allowed to grow up and grow old, too. Just like everybody else. It isn't right that you should have two goes and I should have none. You know it isn't. Please, Grace. Let's swap back. You know it's only right. You know it. Please."

"Oh look!" she crowed, "Granny's crying. Poor old Granny's crying. What a sad old granny she is!"

"Grace!" I pleaded. "Please don't leave me like this! Grace!"

"Don't worry," she said. "It shouldn't be for long. With a bit of luck you might soon be dead. Otherwise I'd have left things a bit longer. But no. Best to be on the safe side, I thought. Best to make a move while the going's good."

She turned a last cartwheel and headed for the door.

"I'm starving," she said. "I'd forgotten how hungry being young can make you. I think I'll have some crisps! I wasn't allowed them when I was old. But now I'm going to have two bags!"

"Grace," I cried, "please, no! Don't go, don't – Grace!"

She paused in the doorway and turned to glare at me with venom and hatred in her heart.

"Never call me that again," she said. "That's *your* name now. *You're* Grace, see. And *I'm* Meredith. And don't forget it, or I'll twist your ears. You'd better remember to do as I say, too. I may be the child now, but I'm still in charge. I'm younger and fitter and stronger than you. So you'd better not cross me. You'd better do exactly as I say. Because I'm not just younger – I'm evil, too. I'm capable of doing terrible things that you couldn't even dream of. And you don't want to find out what they are, Granny, believe me. So you have a good cry, and then you get yourself up to bed. Take the stairs slowly, if you want some advice. And mind you don't fall. Oh, and you'll need to take your glasses off and put your false teeth to soak in a tumbler. And don't forget to put your frumpy old granny's nightie on. And don't be too shocked when you see how saggy and wrinkled you are when you take off your clothes. You'll get used to it. You've got no choice. Have you? So night-night, Granny. Thanks for the body, It's a really nice one. It's so tall and willowy. And it fits a treat."

She left the room, cackling with laughter, slamming the door behind her. When she had gone, I sat on the sofa and I buried my head in my poor, sore, wrinkled hands. I noticed that the skin on them was marked with the dark spots of age, as thin and dry as a fallen leaf.

And then I cried and cried, as though grief would never be over, and I would cry for the remainder of all time.

Only how much of that was there left?'

6

Marmalade and Jam

'I remember making my way up the stairs that night. How long it took me. How slow, heavy and breathless I felt. Normally I would run up, two or three steps at a time. But now I had to pause to rest. My heart pounded. My false teeth rattled in my mouth. My glasses slid down my nose and I had to push them back to be able to see. Even my hearing wasn't so sharp. Sometimes things seemed muffled and far away. But I pulled myself together and dragged myself up to what was now my room, because Grace – Grace in my body – had announced that she was taking my old room over. So I had to have hers.

"The decor's so much more suitable for a younger person, don't you think? An old fuddy-duddy like you needs darker colours and big, horrible, flowery carpets and gloomy wallpaper. Well, you've got them – in your 'new' room. And anyway, you'll want to be nearer the toilet, won't you, in case you have to get up in the night. Ha, ha!"

So I had to move into her room and become the old person in the house. I was the old lady, I was the adult now. Yet I wasn't really an adult at all. I was still a child, and Grace continued to control everything. She said what to do, and kept charge of the money, and looked after the cheque book and everything else.

"We're just going to carry on as normal," she said. "So that nobody will ever suspect. You're going to do the shopping and the cooking and look after the house and smile at the neighbours, same as usual. And I'm going to go to school and pretend to be a stupid schoolgirl who doesn't know a thing. Nobody's going to have the slightest idea. And don't try to tell anyone about this either. For a start, they'll never believe you. They'll think you're just a stupid old crackpot and stick you in a home. A rotten, stinky, old old-folks' home. And you'll have to share a room with somebody who dribbles and makes smells, until you start to dribble and make smells yourself. And you'll never get out again. So just be careful."

What she said frightened me. It really did.

"Yes, we're carrying on as normal for a while, just till the end of this term, see," she said. "Then we're going to sell up and move to a different area, where people don't know us and no one's going to go smelling any rats. Because I might have your body now, but that doesn't mean I've got your creepy-crawly, goody-little-two-shoes, cry-baby personality in it. Sooner or later some interfering busybody at your school is going to start to wonder about me. They're going to wonder why I've changed my attitude and why I'm not some creepy two-shoes any more. And we don't want that, do we? We don't want some do-gooder coming round and asking questions, and getting interested in what doesn't concern them. So that's why we're going to move house and I'm going to go to a new school – where I can be *me* and where I don't have to pretend to be some ghastly little 'Please, Miss, me Miss, I know the answer, Miss!' sort of girl all the time. Got it?"

What could I do but nod my head and meekly answer, "Yes, Grace. Whatever you say."

"That's another thing," she snapped. "Don't ever call me Grace when there's anyone around. I shan't tell you again. I'm Meredith now. You're Grace. You're the old fogey and don't forget it."

"No, Gr— that is, no Meredith," I said.

I felt as if I was talking to myself. Which in a sense I was.

"Good," she grinned. "That's better. Now fetch me some more toast!"

We were sitting at the breakfast table. Normally, Grace would get the breakfast and I would get ready for school. Now it was the other way round. Well, no, that's not quite true. To an outsider, everything would have seemed just as it was before. There was no variation to the routine as far as an outsider would have been concerned – it was just a girl and an old lady, carrying on as normal. But for all that everything looked the same, for me the whole world had turned itself inside out.

I made her the toast. She crunched at it and then started to snigger.

"Wait till I tell Briony," she said.

I looked at her, curious. She had never mentioned Briony before.

"My sister," she said. "An old woman too, just like I – just like *you* are. We had a bet on. As to who would be first to find a stupid girl whose body they could pinch. Looks like I won. Wait till she sees me.

76

She won't half be jealous. She's eighty-five if she's a day. I must give her a ring later, tell her the good news. Now pour me some more orange juice and be quick about it, or I'll whack you on the head with this cereal spoon and then I'll stick this fork up your nose and twist it for good measure."

It soon became clear that Grace was nothing but a bully. She probably always had been inside, but had been too weak and frail to show it. But now that I was old and defenceless, she made threats all the time about what she would do to me if I didn't do precisely as she ordered.

I went to the fridge, opened the door and leaned over to get the juice.

"Ohhh!" I cried.

"What's up, Grandma?" Grace sniggered. "Got a twinge in your back? I really do sympathize. I know just how you feel. I used to suffer from a bad back myself. But then I managed to find a cure for it. It's called 'Someone else's body'. I'd recommend it. Only it's not available on prescription, I'm afraid. You just have to try to get one for yourself. Perhaps you should try the January sales when they come round, or a second-hand shop, or a car boot sale. They might have one. Or if not, there's always the cemetery. Ha, ha, ha! You could dig yourself up a new body. It couldn't be in much worse condition than the one you've got."

I didn't say anything. I didn't want her to know how much I was hurting inside. Wasn't it enough that she had stolen my body? Wasn't that misery enough for anyone? Why was she so unpleasant, so vindictive?

Well, because she was a witch, I suppose, and taking delight in the misery of others came naturally to her. She simply couldn't be anything other than the nasty piece of work she was.

I topped up the orange juice in her glass.

"Thanks Granny," she said. "Now crack on with another piece of toast for me – plenty of butter on it and a decent spread of honey. Then pack my books and get my games kit ready. I don't want to be late for school, do I? And while you're doing that, you can fill me in on some facts and info, and tell me all I need to know. What're the names of the girls in your class? Where do you sit? What do you do at playtime and what kinds of things do you talk about? Stupid, girly stuff, I suppose. Oh well, can't be helped. I've done it once and I can do it again, and it's only a week or two till the end of term, and then we'll be moving and I can be off to a new school where I can be myself and just ignore everybody.

"It takes so long to grow up though, doesn't it? So flipping long. It's just all so tedious, so immensely boring having to be a schoolgirl and waiting for time to go by. I've got to wait until I've been in this body for thirteen months, thirteen weeks, and thirteen days. Thirteen, you see – the witch's lucky number. And then it's mine for ever, and you can never get it back. And then all my wonderful powers return, and you're in big, big trouble. I'll turn you into a slimy slug, and empty a packet of salt on you. Or maybe I'll turn you into a mouse, and throw you over the wall of the cats' home."

I stared at her. She froze in mid-gulp. She knew that she had said too much. So that was it. She couldn't

78

get her full witch's powers back until thirteen months, weeks and days had gone by. Until then – I presumed – she was no more of a witch than I was. There was nothing she couldn't do that I couldn't. But almost as if she could read my mind, she flashed me a sly look of pure malice and evil.

"Don't get any ideas, Granny," she said. "I may have to wait a year or so before I can do any proper witchcraft. But I can do plenty of other things. You don't need witchcraft to be nasty you know. Especially to old people who aren't so quick on their pins. Why, if I was a really unpleasant person, I might even do something nasty now, just to teach you a lesson, something like—"

She looked around the breakfast table. She caught sight of the open marmalade jar.

"Yes, something like – smearing marmalade all over your hair."

And before I could stop her – before I even knew what she was doing – she grabbed the marmalade jar, put her hand into it, scooped out a large clot of thick-cut marmalade and slapped it smack bang on to the top of my head. And then she rubbed it in.

She stood back to admire her handiwork.

"Oh, *much* better, Granny!" she sneered. "*Much* better! You've got some colour in your hair now! Why, you look ten years younger. All you need now is a little more colour in your cheeks. A bit of pink – or some *red*!"

At that she grabbed the pot of raspberry jam, took out a large dollop, rubbed it on to both of her hands and then slapped it right on to my cheeks.

"*Much* better! Much, *much* better!" she yelped.

"Fifteen years younger now! Why, aren't you remark-able for your age, Granny. Such ruddy cheeks, such glowing auburn hair! Aren't you just so *spry*, so *young* looking, so *beautiful*, so very, very *sticky*!"

I thought I was going to cry again. But no. I just felt cold, beyond tears. I only felt a cold, cold anger. I knew that there was no point in trying to retaliate, not there, not then. I was too old and weak and feeble. She was the stronger, that was all there was to it. But another day, another time. Somehow, some-where. I would give her her own medicine back. One day. If I could. Quite how, I didn't know. But if there was a way, I would find it. I hadn't survived so much unhappiness to be destroyed by someone like her now.

So I didn't cry, I didn't shout, or plead or beg. I just left the room and let her get on with her breakfast. I went slowly up to the bathroom on my old legs and got myself into the shower and washed my hair.

It broke my heart to see my old body, so thin and frail. My very bones seemed brittle. All the youth and firmness of my limbs had gone. So this was old age, I thought. This is what it is like when you cannot even pretend to yourself that you look nice or pretty any more.

Not that that was bad. I didn't think that. It's not wrong to grow old. Looks aren't everything, there's character, too. And it can't be helped. It's that or die. It's one or the other. I wouldn't have minded being old if I had lived my life first. That was why I cried to myself as I stood in the shower, my tears and the water running down over my thin and wrinkled skin. I cried because I had never been a teenager, because I had never held hands with anyone or been in love. I cried for the world I had never seen, the places I would never go to, the friends I would never have. Maybe one day I would have had children of my own. But not now, not now. And I cried for them, too.

By the time I was clean and dry and dressed again, you would never have known I'd been crying. That was something I didn't want Grace to see. I wouldn't give her the satisfaction. My white hair was clean, my frumpy old dress was ironed. Underneath it I had on a clean pair of big, old bloomers and on my legs were medicated support stockings, to help with my varicose veins and my poor circulation. On my feet were a pair of clumpy but sensible shoes – I needed them for my corns and bunions and my ingrown toenails. I'd noticed that my toenails were ridged and gnarled and yellow looking, like bits of fungus around the roots of trees.

I made sure my teeth were in straight (I'd put them in the wrong way round to start with, and had got the top set mixed up with the bottom). I gave my glasses a polish with the towel, and then went back downstairs.

Grace was dressed in my school uniform. She was putting my school shoes on and getting my bag ready.

"Oh, one thing, old-timer," she said. "You'll have to carry on doing my homework. I wouldn't want you to miss out on all the pleasures of childhood, so you still get to do the homework, see. Now get my games kit ready, like I said, as it's netball today, isn't it, if I remember correctly? And don't you go steering me wrong or telling me lies or giving me any false

81

information. Because if you do and I find out, it won't just be a drop of marmalade when I get back, it'll be a whole pot of treacle. And I won't just rub it in your hair, I'll make you drink it, along with a bottle of disinfectant and a glass of toilet-cleaner. So you know what to expect if you tell any fibs."

So I told her everything she needed to know to pass herself off convincingly as me. I told her what I normally ate for lunch and what position I played in the netball team.

Then she went. But before she did she looked around the kitchen, and on seeing a painting of mine up on the wall, a painting I'd done ages ago of the house and the garden and which she had once pretended to like – in fact, it was she who had put it up there – she walked over and tore it down, then she screwed it up and threw it into the bin.

"We won't need to look at that rubbish any more, will we!" she said.

With that she went to school, slamming the door behind her and shouting, "Be sure to keep the place tidy, Granny! And get something nice for tea! Like chips!"

So there I was, left to look after the house, like some elderly Cinderella, berated by an Ugly Sister. Only the Ugly Sister was young and pretty. She wasn't ugly, except inside.

I sat at the kitchen table. My hands were trembling and my heart seemed to be fluttering like a bird trapped in a cage. I remembered the pills then, that Grace had taken for her circulation and her blood pressure. I found them in a drawer and read the label. *Two to be taken every four hours.*

I went to open the top of the container but I couldn't. My fingers were too weak and stiff. I rummaged around in the knife drawer and found a gadget in there which I had seen Grace use occasionally – a special gadget for getting the lids off things and for unscrewing the tops off stubborn bottles.

I got the container open and swallowed two pills. I didn't need any water. I'd always had a good swallow and even though I was in someone else's body now, my swallow was as good as ever. (Some things which you think are purely physical often turn out to be all in the mind.)

I decided to make a cup of tea. Funny as it may sound, I'd never made a cup of tea before, and I was a bit nervous of boiling the kettle. But I managed to boil the water and fetch the tea-bags and make a decent cup of tea without spilling any.

I sat and sipped it slowly, and as I did I thought of my mum and dad.

My dad. My mum.

I felt more tears coming on but I fought them back. This wasn't the time to cry. Now that I was alone and Grace had gone, this was the time to make plans, to try to understand what had happened, and to work out what I could do.

I blew on my tea to cool it. I took a biscuit from the biscuit tin (old ladies can take as many biscuits as they like – they're not limited like children) and I dunked it into the tea. It was easier to eat soft, on account of my false teeth. I took my teeth out and looked at them for a moment, and then I put them back in and ate another biscuit.

What to do? How had it all happened? Grace must have planned it from the word go. She had deliberately gone looking for some poor orphan, someone trusting and desperate for a home, like me. She had played the part of the rich, kindly old lady to fool everyone. She wasn't kind though, maybe not even rich. Perhaps it had all been pretend, borrowed money and bouncing cheques.

So she had gained my trust and then she had taken me into her confidence, shown me how to leave my body, how to fly around the room and out into the world. But only in order to steal my body. And now that she had it . . .

But wait. She still *needed* me, like she said. She was still only a girl. She still required an adult to be there, to front for her, to give a semblance of normality. Because otherwise she would be taken into care. She'd be back in the Care Home, the way I was, and she wouldn't want that.

So, yes. She might be younger and stronger and able to bully me, but she still needed me. For a while.

My heart fluttered again. It was an odd, disconcerting sensation, as if it couldn't beat properly. It ticked erratically, like a clock with hiccups.

Then I understood.

The heart. Her heart. My heart now.

Grace had been so anxious to swap bodies because she had been afraid that her heart might not last. She had been afraid that she would die before the exchange could take place.

She had been afraid that she might die.

That *I* might die, now!

84

A cold sweat formed on my brow. My hands began to shake again. I took up the mug of tea to calm myself, but I was trembling so much I spilled tea all over the table.

Thump-a-thump-a-thump-a-thump-a-hic-hic-hic-hic. And then mercifully, once again – thump-a-thump-a-thump.

My old heart steadied. It was best to stay calm. The more upset I got the more irregularly it beat, the more hiccups and stutters there were.

I was going to die!

Thump-a-hic-a-hic-hic-hic – No I wasn't. I could live for years. I wasn't that old. Only eighty-one or so. (Hadn't that been what Grace said she was when I made her that birthday card?) Well, that was no age, no age at all. Eighty-one was still young in a lot of places. (I was sure I'd read that somewhere, or maybe we'd done it in geography.) Some old ladies lived to be a hundred, a hundred and twenty, a hundred and fifty some of them, and they could still do handstands and ride round on donkeys. I was sure I'd heard that. They lived on goat's milk and yoghurt. Well, that was all right. I had years ahead of me. Years and years in which to get back my rightful body.

Maybe I should report what had happened. I could go to the police, the authorities, ring up ChildLine, tell someone in a uniform, go and see Help The Aged even, and explain all about my situation.

Pit-a-pit-a-pit-a—

It would get sorted out. Of course it would. It would all be sorted out in no time.

Thump-a-thump-a—

Calm again. That was better. But then the truth

85

hit me. Who was I fooling? Myself. Myself alone. That was who. No one would believe me. Ever! Not a single soul in the whole wide, immense and limitless universe would ever believe me. I was trapped in this body for ever. Until the day I died. And that day could be any day. Today, tomorrow, the next day. Within the next hour.

Hic-a-hic-a-hic-a-pit-a-pat-a-brrrrrrrrrrrrrrrrr!

I must have fainted. When I awoke my head was on the table and the dregs from a knocked-over tea mug were dripping on to the floor. I got a cloth and mopped the mess up. What was it Grace had said again? Oh yes. *"And you be sure to keep the place tidy! And get something nice for tea!"*

Then I'd better get it done. Or she'd only get nasty and unpleasant again, and I didn't want to give her any excuse for that.

I went to the hall and found Grace's coat on the peg. It was a dowdy old lady's coat, shapeless and woolly, a bit like a sack with pockets, a depressing drab brown colour, and it smelt musty, the way the gardens smell in the rain.

In the inner pocket I found a purse with some money in it – enough to buy food for tea. I supposed that when the money ran out I would have to ask Grace for more. She would have to use her cash card. Only she knew the number. I was just a child. I didn't have one.

By the door was an old lady's shopping trolley, made out of some red tartan material and with two squeaky wheels. I felt in the coat pockets for Grace's door keys. Then I buttoned up my coat, put on a woolly hat – shaped a bit like a flowerpot – wheeled the trolley outside, pulled the door behind me, and set off to the shops.

As I made my way along the street, some of the neighbours said hello.

"Good morning, Miss Grangefield."

Grace Grangefield. That was who I was.

"Good morning," I said back, and slowly went on my way. My corns hurt, my bunions were giving me jip. I wished I had brought my stick.

"Poor old soul," I overheard someone say. "She's past it, really."

At the road junction I waited for the little green man before I crossed. But I made such slow progress that the little green man was turning back to a red one before I'd even got to the other side.

An impatient motorist blasted his horn and shouted something rude out of his car window. It sounded like, "Get a move on, granny!"

I turned and glared at him.

"Don't you be so rude!" I heard my old voice say. "Or I"ll come over there and punch your head in."

That was me, Meredith talking. The motorist looked quite shocked for a second, at the thought of this harmless old lady threatening to give him a hammering. Then he started to laugh.

"Go on, you old boot," he said. "Get off the road before you have an accident and swallow your dentures."

He put his foot down and screeched past me, almost sending my shopping trolley flying.

Finally, I made it to the pavement. I rested by the kerb, holding on to the crossing post for support. A woman with young children passed by.

"I saw that," she said. "People like him, they've got no manners. Are you all right, love?"

"I'm fine," I said. "I'll be OK. Thank you."

She and her children went on their way. "What was wrong, Mum?" I heard one of the children ask.

"The poor old lady couldn't get across in time," the mother said.

Poor old lady.

A day ago I had been a young girl. Full of youth and strength and hope and vitality.

Now I was just a poor old lady.

Poor old lady.

That was me.

And the me I had been? That was somebody else now. Who went to school in my place. And when the term finished, it was just as Grace had said. We moved house and she started a new school – *this* school – where she could "be herself" and not have to pretend to be me.

So here we are. And that's my story, Carly. Thank you for listening. You're the first and only person I've ever told it to. It's so good just to share it with somebody. I know that you probably can't help me. I realize that you probably don't even believe me. I don't suppose I'd believe it either, if I were you. But it's true just the same. The Meredith you know isn't a girl, she's a witch, just waiting to grow up and to start her evil again. And what will happen to me then, I really don't know. She says she's going to put me into a home, where I'll be lonely and forgotten until the day I die. But I'd rather be dead really, than go on for years and years like this.

If only you could help me, Carly, if only you

could. Though I don't suppose you can. Or anyone
can. But at least you've listened to my story. And
that's something. That's a help in its own way. It
really is.'

7

Carly Again

Well, once again you could have knocked me down with a feather. Or even with half a feather. Or possibly with no feathers at all. I mean, I'm no slouch when it comes to nattering and I can talk non-stop when I really have to – like if it was an emergency, or a matter of life and death. Like if you were at the cinema and somebody collapsed and the cry went up 'Is there a doctor, or anyone who can do a lot of talking, in the house?', well I'd be straight up on to my feet.

But even I was taken aback by the amount of nattering Meredith's granny had done that afternoon in the playground. I'd never known anyone cram so many words into such a short space of time. And all the while she talked, she seemed to be looking around nervously, as if something might happen to stop her getting to the end of her story.

I just gawped. I didn't know what to say when she finally stopped. I'd been sitting there listening to it all, feeling my eyes getting bigger and bigger and my lip sort of curling up – the way your top lip does when you get that 'come off it!' feeling when someone is telling you huge porkies. (Porky-pies, that is, lies, in case you didn't know.)

I mean to say, I'd come across some pretty big fibbers in my time, but I'd never come across top-of-the-class quality lying like this before. And she'd kept such a straight face, too, and hardly batted an eyelid at all.

There were some pretty big fibbers in our school, and they could tell you such convincing stories, with such poker faces, all about how they'd gone to the moon in a spaceship at the weekend, or how their long-dead uncle Horace had suddenly dug himself out of the cemetery and had got a taxi home, and had spent all of Saturday night standing by the back door with his coffin under his arm demanding to be let in to watch the football on TV.

Yes, I'd heard some stories in my time, but this one took the biscuit. If I'd had a biscuit on me just then, I'd have handed it over and said, 'The biscuit is yours. Your story definitely takes the biscuit, and here it is. In fact, you can have the whole packet.'

Sometimes, I think people tell me these sorts of stories because of my red hair and freckles. They do it to keep themselves amused. They see me coming and they think, 'Aye, aye. Here's one of those red-haired, freckled types with podgy bits. We'll have a laugh here. Let's tell her the biggest load of fibs we can think of and see how much of it she'll believe.'

Well, once bitten, twice shy, that's what I say. I maybe had been caught out once or twice in the past, but I was wise to that sort of thing now. I'd had my revenge too. Like when Laura Scot persuaded me to believe that her sister's boyfriend had been born with three arms and a tail. I got my own back by telling her that elephants laid eggs and they built big nests under coconut trees, and sat on the eggs for six months at a time in order to hatch them out.

She went and put all that into her biology homework. (Which served her right for not paying attention during the lesson, if you ask me.) She didn't get very good marks, though. I think they were in the region of nought out of ten. Or maybe it was nought out of twenty, I don't really remember.

But as far as Grace's story went, I didn't know what to say. Someone in your class telling you a big load of porkies and expecting you to believe them is one thing. But an elderly, respectable looking lady, old enough to be your granny carrying on like that is quite another.

You don't really feel you can say, 'Come off it grandma, pull the other one it's got bells on,' to a grown-up. You feel you have to be a bit more tactful than that, and furrow your brow and look serious, and say things like, 'Hmm, most interesting. What a remarkable story.' But all the while what you're really doing is thinking, 'What a great big lying toad,' and you wonder what excuse you can make to get away in a hurry without seeming rude.

And yet. Call me soft. Call me stupid. But all the same . . . No! I couldn't believe it. Could I? No!

But then again – it was a fair enough story in some ways, and it had passed the time. But she didn't really expect me to swallow any of it, did she?

No, of course not! She was just having a tease. Only – she wasn't. I could see it in her face. Whether I believed her story or not was, in a way, not important. The important thing was that *she* believed it. And if *she* believed it, it could only mean one of two things. Either that she was completely and utterly round the bend. Or—

'Granny! I hope you haven't been bothering Carly while you've been waiting. What have you been taking about?'

Meredith's sudden appearance came as a shock to us both. She'd somehow crept up on us, stealthy and silent. I spun round. There she was behind me, standing with her bag and her books. In her hand was a copy of the play which she had been rehearsing with Mr Constantine. I could see some of the lines highlighted in yellow. That must have been her part.

'Hi, Meredith,' I said. 'Your granny's been keeping me entertained. How did the rehearsal go? I'm in the play myself, you know. Third Squirrel, that's me. Mr Constantine said I've got to practise eating nuts with both hands, the way squirrels do, so that it'll look convincing on stage.'

But she wasn't listening. She wasn't looking either. Not at me. She was staring at Grace, her grandmother, with a cold, hard stare, as if trying to drill into her mind.

'Are you all right, Granny?' Meredith said. 'Were you surprised to see me? You look as if you've seen a ghost.'

I turned to look at Grace. Meredith was right. The old lady looked pale and petrified – terrified even. Only what was she afraid of? Not Meredith, surely? She had no cause to be afraid of Meredith. Unless . . . unless her story had been true.

No.

No.

'Oh, hello, Meredith, dear,' Grace said. 'You're

93

ready then? You surprised me. You finished earlier than I thought.'

'But I told you not to get here until four o'clock, Granny. I *told* you that I'd be late today.'

'Did you?' the old lady said uncertainly. 'Then I must have forgotten. I came at the usual time—'

'Really?' Meredith said. 'That was a shame. You mean you've had to wait all this time? You with your arthritis. Out in the cold. I *am* sorry.'

'It's not cold, Meredith,' I said cheerfully. 'It's quite warm actually.'

She looked daggers at me.

'It's cold when you're old, isn't it, Granny?'

Grace bowed her head and meekly agreed. 'Yes,' she nodded. 'Yes it is, dear. If you say so.'

'So you'll be anxious to get home now, won't you, Gran.'

'Yes, dear. I suppose I am.'

Meredith reached out and took her arm.

'Good,' she said. 'And you'll be more careful in future, won't you Granny, to remember what I told you, and to get to school when I say.'

'Yes, dear,' Grace said. 'Of course. I'm sorry. Anyone can make a mistake or forget . . .'

I looked at Meredith's hand. It was holding Grace's arm tightly. Very tightly. Too tightly. The old lady winced, as if Meredith's nails were digging into her.

'You know I don't like you bothering people, Granny,' Meredith said. 'You know I warned you about that—'

'She wasn't bothering me, Meredith,' I said. 'Not at all. We were having a pleasant chat. And I didn't have anything else to do. I'm waiting for my mum,

94

see. Over there. Look, she's still nattering to one of the other parents, about private and important matters.'

Meredith didn't hear or she just ignored me. Her cold eyes were fixed on Grace's face. The old lady seemed to wither and grow smaller by the second.

'Yes, you know I don't like you to bother people,' Meredith continued, and her grip seemed to tighten around her grandmother's frail wrist. 'Old people tend to ramble. And go on about the past. And the good old days. And sometimes they get things all mixed up, don't they Granny? And they imagine things, and get confused, and they talk all sorts of drivel – don't they?'

'Yes, dear,' Grace said, her voice timid and shaky.

'That's *right*!' Meredith said. 'And sometimes they get so fuddled they can't tell fact from fiction, or what's true from what they've made up. And so they drone on and on, boring everyone they get the chance to talk to. But they only get away with it because other people are too polite to tell them to stop.'

'Oh, but your granny wasn't being boring at all, Meredith,' I said. 'We were having a most interesting chat. In fact she was telling me all sorts of—'

Meredith fixed me with one of her cold, penetrating looks.

'All sorts of *what*, Carly?' she said.

I had been going to say, 'All sorts of interesting stories.' But something stopped me, held me back. I was suddenly afraid. Not for myself – for Grace. I looked at her arm. Meredith was still holding on to it and her nails – though I could have been mistaken – seemed to be digging in, really tightly.

'All sorts . . . of . . . things,' I said vaguely.

'Really? What sorts of *things*? Stories, maybe?'

'No, not really,' I lied. 'She was just telling me . . . about . . .'

What? What could I say? What, I suddenly thought, if Grace *had* been speaking the truth? I knew it wasn't really possible. But say, for argument's sake that Meredith *had* stolen her body, that the girl standing before me *was* a witch, and that the old woman next to her really *did* have the mind and soul of a young girl the same age as me.

Just say it was true. Just say. Then how did I answer Meredith's question? Without getting the old woman into deep and enormous trouble when she and Meredith were alone? How could I reply to that question without instantly betraying her? To hesitate much longer would be as revealing, and as much of a betrayal, as giving the wrong answer. What could I say?

'Football!' I decided. 'We were talking about – football.'

Meredith looked at me as if I had gone mad.

'You were talking about *football*?' she said incredulously.

'Yes,' I nodded. 'I started it and your granny was telling me that in the old days, footballers used to wear very long shorts.'

Meredith looked from me to her granny, then back to me again.

'Long shorts?' she said. 'Long shorts!'

The long shorts thing was something anyone of any age might know. I knew because I'd seen a photo in a book. It wasn't a very clever answer, but it might do.

It maybe left doubt in Meredith's mind, and that was the main thing.

'Carly! Time to go!' My mum was calling. She'd finished talking at long last.

'Don't dawdle, Carly!' she yelled. 'We do have a home to go to and a meal to get ready, you know.'

That was rich. It wasn't me doing the dawdling. It was her. I'd been ready to go home ages ago. And now she was making out it was all my doing and it was me holding everyone back. But that's parents for you. They'll always try to blame you for what they've done themselves.

'Bye, Meredith,' I said. 'See you tomorrow.'

I turned to her granny.

'Bye—' I felt somehow that I couldn't say 'Bye, Grace'. Using an old lady's first name like that just didn't seem right. So I just said, 'Bye . . . eh . . . bye . . . nice to talk to you.'

I picked up my bag and hurried over to where Mum was waiting at the gate. As we left the playground, I glanced back at Meredith and her granny and gave them a brief wave.

Meredith had her bag in one hand, and with her other had a firm grip on her granny's wrist. When I waved, I suppose Meredith felt obliged to wave back, or it would have seemed peculiar not to. So she let go of Grace and waved her hand in the air. But as she did, I saw something very strange – her nails were red, almost as if she had been painting them with nail varnish. I was too far away to be absolutely sure of what I had seen. Maybe it was my imagination, maybe not. But I also thought I saw red marks around the wrist of Meredith's granny. It was almost as though Meredith had been gripping her grandmother's arm so tightly that her fingernails had dug into her and had drawn blood.

But she wouldn't have done a thing like that. You wouldn't do a thing like that to a frail old lady, to your own grandmother. Would you?

'Carly! Come on!'

I took Mum's hand as we walked along. Mum's hand was firm and strong. Her skin was smooth. There were no age spots or deep wrinkles in it or anything like that. Then I looked at her face. No real lines there either. Just one or two, but nothing serious.

Then I thought, *One day she'll be old. One day my mum will be old, too. Just like Meredith's granny. Just like everyone's granny.*

And I felt sad that my mum, who was so nice and pretty, really – prettier than me as she didn't have the red hair or the freckles or the podgy bits, they all came from my dad – I felt sad that she should have to grow old.

I gave her hand a squeeze.

'Mum,' I said. 'You're not to worry, you know. I'll look after you when you're old.'

She gave me a funny look. 'Carly,' she said, 'whatever made you say that?'

'Nothing,' I said. 'Just thinking.'

She didn't say anything for while. We just walked in silence. But as we came to the pedestrian crossing, she squeezed my hand back.

'Thank you, Carly,' she said. 'Thank you.'

And as we waited for the lights to change, she took her tissue out and blew her nose.

Grown-ups can be funny sometimes if you ask me.

All the way home, I kept thinking of the story that Meredith's granny had told me, how absurd and ridiculous and impossible it was and how it couldn't really be true, not in a million, trillion years.

But then the red marks on Meredith's fingernails would come back to me, and the red weals on her grandmother's wrist. Only I knew I couldn't really have seen that. I was too far away. It had been my imagination,

I couldn't get it out of my mind though. Not the story, nor the red fingernails, nor the marks like spots of blood. I thought about it for the rest of the day. I was still thinking about it when I fell asleep. Even then there wasn't any real escape, for I dreamed about it, too. And later, I dreamed of flying. I dreamed that I had floated up to the ceiling, and was looking down on myself lying there in my own bed. When I woke, I tried to do it, to project myself from my body, as Grace had described. But I remained earthbound. Nothing happened. I stayed right where I was.

8

Meredith's Version

Meredith got more friendly after that. She started asking after my health. I never like it when people start asking after your health. You feel they're only doing it in the hope that you might have something nasty that will finish you off by the end of the week.

I don't like it much, either, when people start asking after your pocket money, or your sweets, or what you might have in your lunchbox. I feel they're only making enquiries for their own reasons and they're not really concerned about you at all. They don't have your best interests at heart. Meredith pretended she did, mind, and she seemed almost genuine. But I was suspicious.

Anyway, as I say, Meredith became more friendly and chatty then – but not towards everyone, just towards me. She ignored all the other children in class the same as she always did, except when she *had* to speak to them, of course.

I wondered if maybe her grandmother had talked to her and had maybe said something like, 'Meredith, you should try to be friendly with that nice Carly, the one with the attractive red hair and the cute freckles.'

Or maybe Meredith had reasons of her own for wanting to get more friendly.

It started the following day, the morning after Grace had told me that fantastic story about how she was the real Meredith, trapped in an old woman's body, and how Meredith was a witch.

Meredith came up to me at break-time and started to chat about nothing in particular, asking me how I was and then saying my hair looked nice today and had I done something special with it? And where had I bought those shoes? And all the kind of stuff that people say to you when they're trying to butter you up like a piece of toast and get you to drop your guard.

I didn't mind though. The two of us standing there talking, it was almost like having a special friend of your own.

After a while, Meredith mentioned her granny.

'I hope she wasn't bothering you too much yesterday, Carly,' she said.

'No, no. Not at all.'

'I can't imagine what she said,' Meredith went on. 'I know she's inclined to ramble.'

Well, she may have been fishing, but I kept my mouth shut and didn't take the bait.

'I suppose I should have warned you, really.'

'Warned me?' I said. 'In what way?'

'About my gran,' Meredith said. 'You see, I try to hide it from people because I'm worried that if I don't, then she could be taken away and put into an institution. And it may sound selfish, but if that happened to her, what would become of me? I'd be put into care as well.'

I bit my lip and kept quiet, and waited for her to go on.

'It is worrying, you see,' Meredith continued, looking serious and concerned. 'There's only the two of us and I've nobody else to confide in, but I'm certain that her mind is going.'

'Oh?' I said. 'How do you mean?'

'It's just not what it was,' Meredith said. 'In all sorts of ways. She's grown very forgetful. It worries me sometimes. I'm afraid she'll go out and leave the fire burning, or the gas on. And she tells the most fantastic stories . . .'

'What kind of fantastic stories?' I asked, as casual as you please.

'Oh, all sorts,' Meredith sighed. 'Things about when she was a little girl. Things that almost sound just about possible. And then she'll go a step too far, and you think, "Oh, no. Come off it. *That* could never have happened."'

I nodded solemnly.

'I know what you mean,' I said. 'My dad's a bit like that. He's always coming out with stuff and trying to get you to believe it. He says it all with a straight face too, until you finally believe him, then he teases you for ever listening to him in the first place. Then, as soon as you've forgotten about it, he'll go and do it again.'

But Meredith didn't seem much interested in my dad's porkies.

'No, this is different, Carly,' she frowned. 'This is much more serious. Granny isn't doing it for a joke. She isn't even aware she's doing it. I don't think she knows what she's saying half the time. It is so very worrying. I don't know what to do.'

'You can talk to my mum about it if you want,' I

offered. 'If you want a grown-up to speak to. I'm sure she'd be glad to give you some advice. Tell her it's a private matter. She likes them.'

'No, no,' Meredith said hurriedly. 'No, I won't do that, Carly. Thank you all the same. I'd rather that as few people knew as possible. I'll just try to keep an eye on Gran and look after her myself. I don't want her to be taken away. So please don't mention it to anybody else. Not even to your mum. You know the way grown-ups talk to one another. It would soon get out and then maybe somebody from the Council might come round and take Gran away.'

She seemed genuinely anxious, so I promised not to tell anyone about her gran losing her marbles.

'The strangest thing about it all,' Meredith said, 'is that I almost spend more time looking after her now than she does looking after me. It's almost as if I've become the adult and she's become the child.'

My mouth fell open. She must have seen me gawping.

'What's the matter, Carly? Are you all right? You look shocked. Was it something I said?'

'No, no,' I insisted. 'Not at all.'

I looked down at my hands. I realized that I had been twisting a piece of tissue round and round. I had wound it really tight and was nearly strangling one of my fingers.

'Meredith,' I asked, as innocently as I could. 'These stories and things that your gran makes up – what kind of stories are they?'

'Oh, everything,' Meredith said. 'You name it. All sorts of fantastic stuff. Stories about when she was a girl. Stories about how she used to be rich and live in a big house. Stories about ridiculous things like elves and fairies and wizards and witches and—

'Witches?' I said.

Meredith looked at me.

'Yes. Witches.' But the expression on my face must have seemed so ridiculous that she started to laugh. 'Oh no, Carly!' she giggled. 'You believe in them, too!'

'No, I don't!' I denied.

'You do! I can see it in your face.'

'I do not,' I said. 'Witches and wizards and all that sort of stuff – that's for nursery school. Honestly. Fancy thinking I believed in that!'

Meredith didn't take her eyes from me.

'Oh, I get it now,' she said. 'Gran was on to you about witches yesterday afternoon. She was on about all *that* again!'

'No, she wasn't,' I said. 'Not at all.'

Maybe she didn't believe me, but she could hardly call me a liar, not right to my face, not if she wanted us to go on being friendly, which was how it seemed.

'Oh well, it was only to warn you,' Meredith said. 'My gran's a really nice old lady, but just be a bit wary, that's all. I should take anything she says with a large pinch of salt – maybe even with a whole packet of salt. She can't really help it. It's what happens to some people when they grow very old. You lose your teeth, you lose your hearing, and then I suppose you lose your marbles. Oh, is that the bell for the end of break? We'd better go back in.'

My mum didn't have any 'important private matters' to discuss with anyone that afternoon. She had 'important shopping' to do instead. So we left the playground early, straight after school finished. I noticed that Meredith walked home on her own. Her granny wasn't there to meet her. One of the teachers saw Meredith leaving and called after her, asking if she would be all right to cross the road.

'I'll be fine,' she said, and without waiting any further, she was away.

I'd have been fine, too. I could easily have got home on my own. Sometimes I felt that Mum met me more in order to talk to the other parents, than to walk me home for my sake.

I wondered about Meredith's granny though, and why she hadn't been in the playground that afternoon. I asked Meredith about it the next day.

'Is your gran all right?' I enquired. 'I didn't see her yesterday.'

'She couldn't come,' Meredith said. 'She was a bit indisposed. I told her that she needn't come to meet me every day. Not if it was getting to be too much for her. I'm old enough to get home on my own.'

'Me too,' I said quickly – and maybe a bit defensively – not wanting her to think that she was the only one growing up. 'So she's a bit ill then is she, your gran?' I asked, trying to make my question sound innocent and free from suspicion.

'Not ill exactly,' Meredith said. 'No. More of an accident, I'm afraid.'

'An accident?' I suddenly had a very creepy feeling.

'Yes,' Meredith said. 'She tripped and fell down the stairs, I'm afraid.'

'Down the stairs?' I said. My mind raced, filling up with all kinds of unpleasant speculation.

'Yes,' Meredith said. 'It's her eyesight, I think. It's not what it was. She must have misjudged the top step, or maybe tripped on the carpet, and down she went – all the way to the bottom.'

'All the way to the bottom?' I echoed, still wondering.

'Yes. Bumpity-bumpity-bump!' she said – almost as if she enjoyed it. 'All the way to the bottom. And then crash, right into the wall!'

'Crash?' I said. 'I hope she wasn't hurt?'

'She was, I'm afraid,' Meredith said. (And to my ears, she sounded rather cheerful about it.)

'Not seriously, I hope?'

'Cuts and bruises,' Meredith said.

'Did you call an ambulance?'

'Didn't like to bother them,' Meredith said. 'I know a bit of first aid, so I patched her up myself.'

'Patched her up – I see. Nothing broken then?'

'Oh no,' Meredith said. 'Nothing broken – at least not *this* time.'

What did she mean? I looked at her carefully. But her face seemed quite innocent.

'When you say "*At least not this time*", are you expecting it to happen again then?'

'You never know,' Meredith said. 'At her age. Obviously, I hope it won't happen. But you never know.'

'I hope you've warned her to be more careful in future,' I said.

'Oh yes,' Meredith said, 'I warned her all right. I warned her good and proper.'

I was going to suggest that perhaps my mum and I could visit the old lady. Maybe take her a cake or a bunch of grapes and a magazine to cheer her up. But Meredith had gone off to join in a game of chase. Which was rather unlike her. She never usually joined in anything. But today was different for some reason. She seemed to be in rather a good mood.

Her granny didn't appear the next day, nor the day after, and then it was the weekend.

On the following Monday though, she was back in the playground in the afternoon, same as usual, waiting to walk Meredith home.

I saw her arrive from where I was sitting in class. I had a seat by the window, which suited me – being a bit nosy – as I could keep an eye on what was going on. Even when nothing was going on, I still liked to keep an eye on it.

She had a black eye. Well, not black exactly, more several shades of blue and several more shades of purple.

Poor old thing, I thought. She took quite a whack there when she fell down the stairs and bashed into the wall.

I saw Meredith glance up from her workbook and spot her granny out in the playground. She kind of winced and gritted her teeth, as if she were very angry about something.

Then the bell went.

We packed our things up and got our coats and headed out to the playground. My mum wasn't there yet. She worked on a Monday and was often late. I went to sit on the wall and wait for her.

As I did, I felt that someone was watching me. I looked round and it was Grace, Meredith's granny. She almost seemed to be pleading with me, with her eyes. She looked lost and desolate, as if her last hope had gone, and that last hope had been me.

'You as well,' her eyes seemed to say. 'So *you* don't believe me either. No one believes me. No one. I'm completely helpless and alone.'

I looked away. I felt terrible, but what could I do? It wasn't my fault that she was getting old and losing her marbles and had started to imagine that her granddaughter was a witch. She couldn't really expect me to believe all that stuff about her body being stolen, and how she was really only the same age as me. Could she?

Meredith appeared. Without a word she poked her granny with her elbow, handed her her backpack to carry, and then the two of them left the playground and made their way along.

They had to pass by me, on the other side of the wall where I was sitting with my back to them. I don't think they realized that I was still there.

They were engaged in an angry conversation. A very one-sided one too, in which Meredith was doing all the talking and Grace was doing all the listening, like it or not.

Meredith's voice was quiet and low, but as sharp as a dagger.

'I told you!' Meredith hissed. 'I told you not to come to the school until that black eye had faded away completely! I don't want busybodies poking and prying and wondering what's going on. So you'd just better listen to me properly in future and do exactly as I say. Or it'll be the worse for you. I'll twist your ear till it hurts, you'll see. And I won't just shove you down the stairs next time either, I'll shove you back up them as well. See how you like that.'

I held my breath and slid quietly down into the playground. They had stopped on the other side of the wall. I wanted to hear every word they said, but didn't want them to see me.

'I'm sorry, Meredith. I didn't mean anything. I just wanted to get out. It's so lonely being by yourself all day—' Grace said.

'Oh, shut up and stop whining,' Meredith told her. Her voice was still low and quiet, but piercing. 'I can do worse than steal your body, you know. I can turn you into a trail of slug slime if you're not careful. You know I'll be able to do it, just as soon as I'm older. And another thing, never let me see you talking to that red-haired, freckle-faced girl again. I don't know what you've said to her, but I'd guess that you've already said too much. Not that she'll believe a word of it. I've told her you're going senile and that you've lost half your marbles. She's too stupid to believe you anyway. She hasn't got the imagination of a worm. But I'm not taking any more chances with you. So you just do as I say. Or you won't just be going round with false teeth, you'll have a bashed-in nose as well. Now come on. Let's get home and you can put the tea on. And I want something decent to eat tonight. So you'd better not burn the sausages again, like you did last time. Or I'll make you eat them all yourself, straight out of the cat's bowl, all mixed up with cat food – the liver and kidney flavour!'

Then they were gone.

The world spun around me. The playground

seemed to be moving under my feet. My heart pounded and my head felt dizzy.

It was true then! It was *true*! Every word that Grace had said to me, the whole story about her being the real Meredith, about the witch stealing her body. It was true.

I looked around frantically wondering what to do. Who could I tell? One of the teachers? The headmaster? One of the parents? One of the other children? A policeman? A traffic warden? The lollipop lady? My mum?

I couldn't tell anyone. They simply wouldn't believe me, the same way I hadn't believed Grace until the truth was stuck under my nose. They'd all think that I was losing my marbles too, and they'd send me away for a good long rest, somewhere quiet out in the country, where I'd have to make baskets and take special pills and have long lie-downs in the afternoons.

I couldn't tell anyone. There was only me. There was only one person who could help the real Meredith. And that was me, Carly Taylor.

I felt horrible. Good and bad and horrible all at once. Panicky too. It was like being the only one at the scene of an accident. Someone was drowning and crying for help, and the only person around to help them was you. Only you weren't such a great swimmer yourself.

I felt out of my depth. But it didn't matter. I had to do something. I had to let the real Meredith know that I believed her now, that I knew she was trapped in an old witch's body and that the old witch was in hers. Even if I could do no more than be a friend to her, then at least I had to do that much.

And as for the witch who pretended to be her, who sat at the desk next to me in class, who always seemed to get all the answers right, who seemed to know everything before it had been explained – I wouldn't let her suspect a thing. I'd carry on being as nice and friendly towards her as ever. Who knows – I might even decide to ask her round to my house.

She wouldn't have an inkling. She'd never know that I knew. Not until it was too late. By the time she realized that I knew the truth about her, she'd be back in her own body, and the real Meredith would be herself again.

Yes. Why not? Why not!

If bodies could be stolen once, then they could be stolen back again, couldn't they? If spells could be made, then spells could be reversed. Surely! It was only a matter of knowledge, as so many things are. It was just a question of finding out how. There was bound to be an answer somewhere. I only had to discover where that was and then to track it down. Astral projection wouldn't work, I knew that, not in a month of Halloweens. I'd never get Meredith to hand her nice new body over just like that. She'd never leave it willingly. She'd have to be evicted.

Ways and means, I thought. There were always ways and means.

But first and most importantly, I had to get a message to the old lady, to let her know that I believed her now, that she wasn't alone any more. And then we would just have to see.

Mum arrived to take me home.

'Carly?' she said. 'Are you all right? You seem a

bit distracted – far away. Are you daydreaming again?'

'No, Mum,' I said. 'Just thinking, that was all.'

'If you ask me, my girl, sometimes you think too much.'

But I didn't agree with that. I don't believe you can ever think too much. The more thinking the better, as far as I'm concerned.

That's what I think.

We walked home. And I carried on thinking. By the time we got to our front door, a plan was already forming in my mind. I had thought of a way to get the real Meredith back into her own body.

'Knowledge is power,' my dad used to say. I knew where the power might be hidden and where the knowledge might be found.

9

The Spell

Time can do all sorts of things. It's almost like a magician. It can turn autumn into spring and babies into children, seeds into flowers and tadpoles into frogs, caterpillars into cocoons, and cocoons into butterflies. And life into death. There's nothing that time can't do. Except run backwards. That's its trouble really, it can only go one way. Time's like water, it can't run uphill.

But in my experience, if you've got a problem of any kind or a wish that won't come true, if you can wait long enough, time may solve the problem for you. Time brings birthdays and Christmas, and they bring presents. Sometimes you do get what you want, if you can only be patient. Which is the hard part.

As I discovered while I bided my time and waited for a chance to talk to Grace on her own, without Meredith being around to overhear.

Meredith watched the old lady like a hawk and guarded her like an Alsatian. I tried to get out of class early to talk to her before Meredith appeared. But Meredith somehow always got out before me. I tried to tell the old lady by looks and glances that I believed her now, that I was on her side and wanted to help and had a plan. But she rarely looked up from the ground. She kept her eyes down and stared at her clumpy old shoes, as if nearly all hope had gone, and what was left was slowly leaking away.

But then I managed to slip her a note as she was leaving the playground with Meredith a few steps in front of her, one afternoon. I pressed it into her hand. Her skin felt so dry and old. It was like a dried leaf. You half expected it to crumble away.

I believe you, my note said. *Come early – on Wednesday, 'Meredith's' rehearsal day. But not to the playground. I'll sneak out. Meet me by the phone box – down by the Lollipop Lady. I'll wait till you can come. Don't let 'Meredith' see this note. From Carly.*

The old lady gave nothing away when I pressed the folded-up note into her hand. She didn't turn round or even glance at me. She was too afraid that Meredith would see her and realize that something was up.

But I saw her slip the note into the pocket of her baggy old coat. I knew that it was safe then and that she would read it and then destroy it as soon as she could. I imagined her getting home and heading straight up to the bathroom saying, 'I have to go to the loo!'

Sometimes you have to go to the loo a lot when you get old, so Meredith wouldn't be suspicious of the old body hurrying up the stairs without even taking its coat off. Then, once the bathroom door was locked behind her, I could picture her reading the note, and how hopeful and cheered-up she'd be. Then she'd roll it up into a ball and flush it away down the toilet. And she wouldn't go back downstairs until she was sure that it had disappeared.

And then she would make plans to sneak out and meet me on the following Wednesday afternoon, while Meredith was acting tall and willowy in the school play rehearsals, with Mr Constantine watching her saying, 'More emotion, Meredith. More emotion!'

He'd said it to me once, and I was only Third Squirrel. But you can't expect much emotion from a Third Squirrel.

'More emotion, Carly!' he said. 'You have to *think* yourself into the part! Think squirrel! Be the squirrel! Live the squirrel! Get right inside the squirrel You've lost your acorns and you may never see them again. So be *emotional*!'

Well, it was all right for him, he was born emotional. How was I supposed to know how a squirrel that had lost its acorns felt? How could I get all emotional over a couple of nuts?

She wasn't there. She was late. I'd sneaked out of the playground while Mum was discussing important matters and I'd gone along the path to the telephone box.

'Do you want to cross the road, love?' the Lollipop Lady asked me, itching to get a bit of lollipop work in. I think she loved holding the traffic up. She used to go as slowly as possible, just to irritate the motorists.

'No thank you very much,' I said. 'I'm waiting.'

'You could cross the road and then come back again,' she offered.

'No thanks,' I said.

Luckily some five-year-olds came along and the Lollipop Lady had some customers.

I waited by the phone box, but there was no sign of Grace. I began to get worried. I'd have to get back to the playground soon, or Mum would come looking for me. Or worse still, Meredith would be out from play rehearsals and—

There she was, coming slowly up the road. She had a walking stick with her, and she tap-tapped her way along. She was plainly trying to hurry, but all the hurry was in her face, there was none in her poor old legs. The more her face tried to hurry, the more her legs seemed to drag.

I ran down the road to meet her.

'What happened?' I said. 'You're late. I thought you weren't going to come. We don't have much time now. They'll be out of rehearsals soon. So listen carefully. There's no time for sympathy or commiserations right now. I am sorry about what's happened to you. But the point is, I believe you now. I overheard what she said and I know she pushed you down the stairs. But listen, I've had an idea – about how to get you back into your body. If I tell it to you, will you be able to remember it?'

The old lady nodded.

'I think so. My mind's not that bad.'

'OK. Now, listen. When you're alone in the house tomorrow, search it from top to bottom until you find that book you told me about, the big thick one with the metal clasps, that one called – what was it again?'

'Necromancy? That one?'

'That's it. See, witches have spells, right, and they can't possibly remember them all, so they must have them written down. There must be one in that book

116

to get you back into your own body. If we only know what it is, we can do it. Don't you think?!'

I was excited. But she didn't seem to share my enthusiasm.

'But what if the spell's not there?'

'It's got to be somewhere. And even if it isn't, there's no harm in looking. At least we'll be doing something. At least there's a *chance*!'

'OK,' she nodded. 'I'll do it.'

'If you find the right spell, copy it and give it to me,' I said.

'How shall I get it to you? Meredith's got her eye on me all the time.'

I had an idea.

'I know!' I said. 'You can post it to me!'

'Good thinking,' she said.

I told her my address and got her to repeat it several times over to make sure she had remembered it properly.

'OK,' I said. 'I'll watch out for a letter from you. We'd both better go now. Rehearsals will be over any second, and if Meredith sees us talking she'll know something's up.'

'Carly! Carly!' It was my mum, standing by the school gates calling my name. 'What are you doing there? I've told you not to wander out into the street!'

'Sorry, Mum.'

'Doesn't matter. Come on now, time to go.'

'Bye, Grace,' I said to the old lady. 'That is . . . Meredith . . . that is . . . well, bye anyway. And find that book!'

I ran to join Mum. The old lady made her way to the school and I saw Meredith come out of

117

rehearsals. And then, as we walked away, I heard their voices, on the other side of the wall.

'You didn't get here early and hang around, did you?' Meredith said.

'No.'

'Didn't talk to anyone?'

'No.'

'Good. Or you'd be in trouble. Come on then. Here's my bag. Let's go.'

'Was that Meredith's granny I saw you talking to, dear?' Mum asked me later as we walked home.

'Em – yes, might have been,' I said.

'She seems a bit lonely,' Mum said. 'Maybe I ought to ask her round one day. What do you think?'

'Yes,' I said. 'Yes, that would be a good idea.'

Further plans were already forming in my mind. Plans within plans and wheels within wheels. It was enough to make your head spin.

I was going to have a sister.

Like the sister I should have had, and nearly did, but only for a little while. I know one person can never replace another. I didn't want or expect that. That wasn't what I meant. No, it wasn't that. It would just make up for it in some way, that was all. The presence of someone else in the house would fill that empty space, soothe that ache, that loss we all felt – me and Mum and Dad, too. And I'd be helping Meredith as well, rescuing her, almost. It wasn't all for me. I'd be helping someone.

The spell came through the post two days later. I'd never had a spell come through the post before.

118

I'd had postcards and birthday cards, but never a spell. It was scribbled in a child's hand, a child of my age. There was a note attached to it. The writing said, *You were right, Carly. I found the book and here's the spell to do it. Some spells you have to be a proper witch to do, but others anyone can manage, as long as they have the right ingredients and the exact words, and I think this is one of them. But there's a problem, as you will see. Maybe you can think of a way around it. See you next Wednesday, same time or a bit earlier, by the phone box. Signed, your young but old-looking friend, the real Meredith.*

P.S. Thank you for believing me.

I read the spell through, wondering what the difficulty was. It would probably be something we had to get. Something near impossible to get hold of, like some stewed eye of newt or fresh lizard's tongue or lost squirrel nuts or something like that.

But no. Nothing of the sort. You didn't need anything special at all. You just needed to say the words – the exact words – in the way prescribed, and in the presence of the two people whose bodies and souls were to be swapped around.

So where was the difficulty in that? I couldn't see any. I couldn't understand what Meredith meant.

Then I realized what the problem was – co-operation! The witch wasn't going to sit down in any rooms while long spells were read out to deprive her of the young body she had stolen and to put her back into her old one. She'd kick, scream, scratch and spit before she'd let that happen. She'd howl and yell and gouge and fight with everything she had. She'd tear my hair out and Grace's hair out, and maybe even her

119

own hair out and the cat's hair out, too. That was the problem and it was a major problem. There was only one way we could do it. She would have to be asleep. Or unconscious.

How did you get people to be unconscious for a while? There was only one way I could think of. We would have to hit her with a brick.

Hmm.

I considered the brick treatment, but then I saw it was out of the question. The trouble was that to make the witch unconscious, it was Meredith's body I'd have to hit with the brick. Which meant that after the spell, when Meredith was back in her own body, she'd find she had a terrible headache and a great big lump, and possibly even a fractured skull.

So that was no good.

My mum, meantime, still feeling sorry for Meredith's granny, had been as good as her word and had invited them both round for tea one day after school.

'It'll be nice for us all,' she said. 'You can play in the garden with Meredith and I can chat with her granny.'

'Will you have important matters to discuss, Mum?' I asked.

'We might do,' she said. 'You never know.' And she gave me a bit of a funny look, like she thought I was taking the mickey.

I dare say that Meredith would have preferred not to come to our house. She didn't like to get too friendly with anyone. And she liked her granny to get friendly with people even less. She didn't want people like my mum getting too interested in them and

120

asking difficult questions. But it would have seemed rude to refuse.

The afternoon wasn't a great success. Meredith didn't want to play with me much, she just wanted to watch TV or go on the computer. She seemed very interested in the Internet. I left her to browse it on her own. She was probably looking for a website for witches.

I tiptoed off to the kitchen where Mum was getting tea and cakes ready. She and Grace seemed to have run out of conversation and there was an embarrassed silence in the room.

'Meredith's on the computer, Mum,' I said, coming to the rescue. 'Shall I show her gran the garden?'

'Oh, would you, Carly,' Mum said, relieved. 'That would be nice. I'll give you a call when tea's ready. It won't be more than five minutes.'

I led the old lady outside, and we sat on the garden lounger, where nobody could see us.

'Listen,' I said, 'and don't say anything till I've finished. I got the spell you sent me, but I see the problem. She's got to be unconscious and I've worked out how to do it. At first I thought a good hard smack with a brick would be the answer, but that only causes problems of its own. No. Look, we have to slip something into her drink.'

The old lady looked at me.

'But *what*, Carly? I don't have anything to slip into her drink to make her fall asleep. I can't slip a brick into her drink, can I?'

'No,' I said. 'But you can *get* something.'

'What?'

'Sleeping pills.'

121

'Where from?'

'From the doctor.'

'The doctor? But the doctor will never give me sleeping pills. I'm just a . . . a . . .'

I knew what she had been going to say. She had been about to say, *'I'm just a child.'*

But, of course, she wasn't. Not as far as any doctor would be concerned. She would be an old lady with sleeping problems, kept awake at nights by her arthritis. She'd have no trouble getting sleeping pills at all.

'So?' I said. 'Can you do it?'

She nodded her head.

'I think I should be able to get them,' she said. 'And then what?'

'Then you ask me round to your house,' I said.

'What? But Meredith—'

'My mum's asked you round. It'll seem funny if you don't ask us back. Even Meredith'll realize that. And all she wants to do is pretend to be normal and not arouse any suspicions. So invite us round to your house and I'll try to leave my mum at home. When I'm there, I'll play with Meredith while you get some tea ready. You crush up some sleeping pills well in advance, and while we're playing, you dissolve a couple of them into Meredith's drink. Not *too* many, mind. Just enough to put her to sleep for a while. Because don't forget that once the spell's been done, you'll be back in your own body. You don't want to be asleep for weeks in it, do you?

'Anyway, you slip the sleeping potion into her drink and then you call us in for tea. Meredith drinks her milk – or whatever you've put the sleeping pills into – she falls asleep right there at the table with her face in her jelly, or whatever. Then straight away we get the spell out. I recite the spell. In a couple of seconds you're back in your body and she's in yours.'

'Won't she be mad, though?' the old lady said. 'She'll be back in this old body and she'll be wide awake and hopping mad. And I'll be asleep. There'll just be you and her until I wake up.'

I hadn't thought of that. She might try to strangle me. Or hit me with a brick. She would be back in a frail, old body, but there's no telling what people are capable of when they're angry. And she would be. No doubt about that.

'You're right,' I said. 'You'll have to drink some of the sleeping draught as well. Quite a bit. So that Meredith's body will wake up first and then we can both escape.'

Then she asked another question.

'Escape, Carly? Escape to *where*?'

But that one I'd already thought about.

'Here!' I said. 'You come back *here*! Home with *me*!'

'But your parents,' she said. 'Your mum and dad.'

'We'll sort that out in advance,' I said. 'You talk to my mum on the quiet. You say that you're worried about growing old and about your health failing. Say you're concerned about Meredith and what might happen to her if you couldn't look after her any more. Knowing my mum, she'll say Meredith can come and live with us, as I've always wanted a sister. And that can be *you*, see!'

'Yes, but—'

'No buts at all,' I said. 'It'll work like clockwork.

123

And my dad's a lawyer too. If you ask him to, he'll even help you make out a will, saying that you'd like Meredith to come and live with us if anything should happen – that you'd want us to be her guardians, or trustees or whatever. You have to do it. Let's face it. You can't possibly stay with a witch. Not once you've got your own body back. She might try to steal it again. Or do something even worse to you, like turn you into a snake, or a rice pudding with skin on top.'

'Yes, only—'

'It'll be all right,' I said. 'Honest. When that witch wakes up to find herself back in her own body, she'll probably have a fit anyway and need to be taken away in a white van, I should think, to one of those special rooms with padded walls, and where they keep all the bricks carefully locked up so's you can't do yourself any damage. So what do you say? Would you like to come and live with us and be my special friend and sister? What do you think?'

The old lady's hand reached out and took mine.

'I'd like that more than anything, Carly,' she said. 'More than anything in the world.'

'Me too,' I said. 'So that's settled. And don't worry about my freckles – they're not contagious.'

Just then Mum's voice called from the kitchen.

'Ready!' she yelled. 'Carly! Tea's ready!'

'Come on,' I said. 'We'd better go in now and not talk any more. We don't want Meredith getting suspicious. Just remember what you have to do. *One*, go to the doctor for sleeping pills and *two*, speak to my mum about Meredith coming to live with us if anything should happen to you. Oh, and *three* –

invite me round to your house for tea. And *fourth*, whatever you do, don't let Meredith get suspicious. Just carry on as normal. OK?'

'OK,' she said. 'And thank you, Carly. Thank you for believing in me and for all your help.'

'No problem,' I said. 'Now I don't know about you but I'm starving. Let's go in.'

And in for tea we went. Before we could start I had to fetch Meredith from the computer.

'Tea, Meredith,' I said. 'Didn't you hear my mum calling?'

'Sorry,' she said. 'I got distracted.' Then she suddenly looked worried. 'Where's my gran?'

'In the kitchen,' I told her. 'Talking to my mum.'

'Has she been there all the time?' Meredith asked, standing and turning off the computer.

'As far as I know,' I answered. (I don't normally hold with lying, but when there's witches involved, I'm prepared to.)

'Right,' she said. 'Tea, then?'

'Tea,' I nodded. And we went to the kitchen.

Grace hardly ate anything. She had an appetite as tiny as a sparrow's. But Meredith ate like a hog. For all that she was tall and willowy, she couldn't half pack it away. She could wolf it down like nobody's business. And that's one thing I've noticed about witches, they don't half like their grub.

Three or four days later, I saw the old lady in the playground. I couldn't talk to her as Meredith was watching, but when her back was turned, Grace winked at me and mouthed, '*I've got them*,' and she took a little brown glass bottle from her pocket and held it up for me to see.

So she had them. She had been to the doctor's and had managed to get the sleeping pills. (Though to be honest, she was so old and crumbly looking, she looked more like her trouble was staying awake.)

But Grace had been busy, all right. And not just round at the doctor's surgery either, as I was later to find out.

'Your friend Meredith's grandmother rang me up this morning,' my mum said as we walked home from school the following afternoon, 'and I met up with her for coffee.'

The days were getting shorter now and the evenings started early. The pavements were covered in dead leaves. I hated the winter. It wasn't the cold, I didn't mind that. I quite liked getting all wrapped up in layer upon layer, it was almost like being a parcel. It was the dark I didn't care for, and the way the day was over so soon.

I tried not to seem *too* interested in what Mum was saying.

'Oh? Called, did she? And you met up? What was that about?'

Mum looked at me a bit sideways, as if to watch my reaction to what she was about to say next.

'Carly,' she said, 'you know that Dad and I can never have any brothers or sisters for you now?'

I did know. They'd already told me. But I didn't know why, exactly. It was something to do with the way the premature baby had been born. It was too dangerous for Mum to have any more. I think otherwise she would have done, she'd have had loads, and filled the house with them.

'The thing is, Carly – look, let's sit down here.'

We sat down on a bench under a tree. If it was sitting-down news rather than standing-up or walking-along sort of news, it had to be important.

'Carly,' Mum said, 'you know that Meredith's granny, Grace, is quite elderly, don't you?'

Of course I did. Anyone could see that. If she'd got any older, she could even have been worth a lot of money.

'Yes, Mum,' I said. 'What about it?'

'Well, Grace is a little worried about what would become of Meredith if she got too old or frail to look after her. So she asked me—'

I didn't say anything. I didn't want to interrupt. I knew what was coming.

'—She asked me if we would, well, be willing to look after Meredith if anything were to happen – if Meredith could come and live with us – if she could put it in her will that your father and I would become Meredith's guardians. '

'So what did you say?' I asked.

'I said we'd think about it and talk it over and let her know. So what do *you* think, Carly? How would you feel about Meredith coming to live with us if her granny couldn't look after her any more?'

'Yes!' I cried. 'Yes, yes, yes!' Then, not wanting to seem too keen, I tried to tone it down and added, 'That is, I don't mind – if you want – I'm not really bothered one way or the other – it's all the same to me.'

Mum smiled. 'Good,' she said. 'I'll talk to Dad tonight, then. But I suspect his answer will be the same as mine.'

'Which is?' I asked, holding my breath, suddenly

afraid that maybe she wouldn't want another child in the house.

'Yes, of course, Carly! What else? We couldn't leave Meredith to be put into care or to be brought up by strangers, could we? Not when we're here and we've room for her and you'd like to have a sister. We couldn't *not* help, could we?'

'No,' I said, 'of course we couldn't. My feelings precisely.'

And that was more or less it. We both knew that Dad would say the same, but we asked him anyway, out of politeness' sake, so he could feel that his opinions mattered and there was a chance that they might make a difference.

'It's very unlikely that anything will happen to Meredith's granny though,' Dad said. 'You know the saying – *a creaky gate swings long.*'

I didn't.

'What do you mean – *a creaky gate swings long?*'

'It means, Carly, that the oldest, creakiest people who seem most likely to pop off, can often outlast the rest of us, who don't creak quite so much.'

'Hmm,' I said. And I thought to myself – we'll see about that. Once Meredith is back in her own body and the witch is back in hers, we'll see how long the creaky gate swings then. Not long, I don't think. When the witch wakes up and finds she's old again, she might well pass away from the shock.

So there it was. It was all arranged now and all agreed. Meredith could come and live with us. It was all set. We had the plan, we had the sleeping pills, we had the escape route, we had the spell. The only thing we didn't have yet was the invitation for me to go round to Meredith's house, so that we could put the whole thing into operation.

It wasn't long in coming. It arrived the next day. From Meredith herself, unexpectedly enough.

10

Asleep

'Would Carly like to come round for tea and to play one afternoon, Mrs Taylor?'

We were in the playground. Mum was looking round to see where the Parents With Important Matters To Discuss were holding their meeting that day. Meredith's granny was hobbling along the road towards the school gates. She used her walking stick more and more now, and seemed to be getting stiffer and stiffer – the way corpses are supposed to.

Meredith was just behind me as we came out of class. As soon as she saw my mum in the playground, she went over and made the invitation. She made it within earshot, but just the same I felt she should have asked me first. It was up to *me* whether I wanted to go round to her house for tea. Not my mum.

'I'm sure Carly would be delighted,' Mum replied, looking at me for a yes or no. I just shrugged and nodded my head, staying all sort of casual, so that nobody would get suspicious.

'OK,' I said. 'I don't mind. If you like.'

By then the old lady had joined us.

'Is that all right, Gran,' Meredith said, 'will it be OK for Carly to come round to tea one night?'

'I should think so, dear,' she said, in her old granny's voice.

'Only if it's not too much trouble,' my mum hastened to add. (Though I wasn't all that keen on her implying that I was a load of trouble to have round at your house. It's not very nice, is it?)

'No trouble at all,' the old lady said. 'It'll be a pleasure to have her round. I can't imagine Carly ever being any trouble.'

Then, while Meredith and my mum were looking elsewhere, she winked. It was one of those conspirators' winks, that you give to people you are in cahoots with, like when you are planning a bank robbery and at last everything is set, and the big day has arrived.

'Which day did you have in mind?' my mum asked. 'Not today, I'm afraid. Carly has her violin lesson this afternoon.'

I hated that violin. And the lessons. Whenever I played the violin it sounded like somebody torturing a cow. And possibly a pig as well.

'How about Friday?' Meredith asked.

I nodded.

'Fine.'

'Friday, Grace?' Mum asked the old lady.

'Perfect,' she said.

So Friday it would be.

I woke up several times on the Thursday night, thinking about what we had to do the next day and whether we would be able to do it.

It's always a bit like that when there are big things

ahead of you. You know you can do them, but doubts and fears creep in just the same, and they keep you awake as you imagine everything that might go wrong.

But I never once imagined what really *would* go wrong. That possibility didn't cross my mind at all.

I slept in on Friday morning, after all the tossing and turning and waking up and punching the pillow and trying to get back to sleep.

'Carly! You'll be late!' Mum said, banging on my door.

'Coming,' I mumbled, wishing that we could put things off until another day. I didn't feel up to pills and potions and spells and witches. I just wanted to stay in bed.

I wish I had.

But I didn't. I got up and got dressed and put the spell carefully in my pocket. Then I went down to have breakfast and then dragged myself to school.

I couldn't pay attention to any lessons that day. The teacher's words just buzzed around the room like flies. I kept looking at the back of Meredith's head, thinking, *She's a witch. She's a real and actual witch. She's not a girl. She's an old, old witch, a spotty old crone, living in someone else's body. And come tonight, she'll be back where she belongs.*

And do you know, incredible as this may seem, I actually felt sorry for her. I don't know why. I knew she was wicked and what she'd done was wrong. But for a second I wondered if I wouldn't do the same – if I could. If I was old and had the chance to be young again, would I take it? Even if it meant stealing someone else's youth? I didn't know. I hoped that I wouldn't. But I knew that I might be tempted.

Then I thought about how the real Meredith would be able to come to live with us, and I could have a special friend and a sister. I forgot about the witch then. She was simply going to get what she deserved. I reached into my pocket and felt in it for the piece of paper. Yes, there it was, the spell, the one Grace had sent to me.

In a few short hours it would all be over, all said, and all done. But how those few short hours dragged. They went on unendingly, slower than snails, dragging time along behind them, as if it weighed a million tons.

Finally, at last, the bell went. School was over.

Meredith packed her books up and chucked her homework into her bag.

'Ready, Carly?' she said. 'Gran should be waiting in the playground.'

'Ready,' I said.

'Come on, then. Let's go to my house. We'll have some fun. We can go on the computer, watch TV, play in the garden, whatever you like.'

'Great!' I said, trying to sound keen and delighted, so that she wouldn't suspect what was really on my mind.

'Then let's go.'

We walked out to the playground. Knowing that I was going to Meredith's house, my mum wasn't there. Grace smiled when she saw us.

'You run on ahead if you like, girls,' she said, 'and

I'll catch up with you. Not too fast though, and not too far ahead.'

'Oh, Granny,' Meredith snapped, 'don't fuss!'

'I was only—' Grace began.

'Well, don't!' Meredith stopped her. 'Come on, Carly, let's go!'

We went on ahead. By the time the old lady caught up with us we were already back at Meredith's house, playing in the garden. There was a swing there and a climbing frame and a rope ladder attached to the branch of an oak, and even a tree house.

'She has everything,' I thought. 'Meredith has everything.'

So we played for a while and I tried to be friendly and to carry on as if everything was normal. And Meredith did too. Which of course was strange, I now realize, looking back on it. Because she was playing a part too, wasn't she, all along. She was an old witch, playing at being a schoolgirl. Playing at playing, if you like. That was what she was doing. Playing at playing with me.

While we were out in the garden, I looked towards the kitchen window. Grace was inside, getting the tea ready. It wasn't a cooked tea, more a snack one, with cake and biscuits and sandwiches and glasses of milk.

She gave me a small wave from the window, and another of those special winks that conspirators give each other. Then, while Meredith was shinning up the rope ladder to the tree house, I saw Grace take what must have been her bottle of sleeping tablets out. She snipped the end off a capsule and poured the powder out into what was going to be Meredith's glass of milk. It was a tall plastic tumbler, with little red ballet dancers leaping around the rim.

'Come on up, Carly, up into the tree house. Use the ladder. It's quite safe.'

I started to climb. I could still see into the kitchen. Grace opened up a second capsule, then a third. Maybe that was too many? But then I remembered that she had to take some too. They both had to be asleep. Only Meredith's body had to wake up first. The witch was going to be furious when she found herself back in her old body. But hopefully, by then, Meredith and I would be ready to run.

'Come up into the tree house, Carly.'

Come into my parlour, said the spider to the fly.

I climbed. As I did I decided to hang from my knees. Just to see if I could do it. I could. There I was, hanging upside down, everything topsy turvy.

Something fluttered past my eyes.

The spell! The piece of paper with the spell! It had fallen from my pocket.

'Carly! What's that, Carly? You've lost something from your pocket. Looks like a piece of paper. Shall I jump down and get it?'

'No! No – thanks all the same. I can manage.'

I right-sided myself and climbed down the rungs of the rope ladder to retrieve the folded paper from the ground. Two shiny eyes looked down on me from the darkness of the tree house.

'What is that, Carly? What did you drop?'

I couldn't think. My mind was blank and nothing would come. Not like me at all. I was usually so good at making things up on the spur of the

135

moment. 'It's nothing, Meredith, just a – a – just a poem.'

Why did I say that? Why on earth did I say that? It just made it worse.

'A poem? Have you written a poem? I didn't know you wrote poems. I write poems sometimes. Can I see it? Oh, do let me see it, *please*.'

I picked the spell up. The paper was still folded up into its four quarters.

'I'd rather not, actually, Meredith.'

I squinted up at her. All I could see were those two eyes, looking down at me.

'Oh please, Carly, *please*.'

Her voice was wheedling, whiny. Not like I'd heard it before. Not like her voice at all.

'Please, Carly! Oh, *please* let me read your poem.'

'N-no. I'd rather not actually. It's not that I don't want you to – that is—'

'But I thought we were friends, Carly. And friends don't have secrets from each other, do they? Friends trust each other and confide. Please let me read your poem, Carly, please.'

'I will,' I said, 'I promise. But not today. It's personal, see. And not quite right yet in places. There's a few things I have to change. It needs a bit of thought still, that's all.'

'I don't mind. Maybe I can help you with it. Why don't you read it out to me if you don't want me to see it? I don't mind.'

It was like talking to darkness. Darkness with two devil's eyes looking out of it. Two hot coals in a dark, dark cellar. Two glittery hot coals.

'Read me the poem, Carly, please. Miss out the

136

bits you don't want me to hear and read me the rest. Won't you? For me? We are friends, aren't we?'

'Yes,' I said, staring up at the tree house. How come all I could see was those eyes? 'Yes, of course we're friends, only—'

'Unfold the paper, Carly—' The voice didn't seem to be coming from the tree house any more, it seemed to be coming from within my own head.

'Unfold the paper, Carly. Read out the words. Read them out so that I can hear them. Tell me your secret thoughts. Then we can be better and closer friends. Friends shouldn't have secrets, Carly. They should tell each other everything. All their hopes and plans and dreams. Don't you think? Do read me your poem, Carly. Or maybe I can guess. Maybe I can try to guess what it's about. Shall I try? Do you think I'll be able to do it? Do you think so?'

Rat-a-tat-tat! Rat-a-tat-tat!

Saved. By the window. It was Grace, tapping on the glass, beckoning, calling.

'Tea, girls! Tea's ready! Come in and wash your hands!'

I put the paper safely away in my pocket.

'Meredith! Your gran's calling. She says to come in. Tea's ready.'

'Oh, right. OK. Coming.'

Suddenly there she was – all of her, not just two beady eyes. She was shinning down the rope ladder, fast and easy, like an acrobat. Then there she was, right next to me, the fallen paper and the poem apparently forgotten.

'Come on then, Carly. I'm starving. Aren't you? In

fact, I'm always hungry. Sometimes I think I just can't get enough to eat.'

I looked at her. She was a good head taller than me and so slim and willowy. It didn't seem fair. She could eat what she wanted and as much as she liked and stayed slender. I tried not to have too many sweet things, but all I got were podgy bits. But there you are. There's worse things in life than podgy bits.

As I was about to discover.

We went in for tea.

Maybe I should tell you about the spell. I hope you're not expecting too much, for it was quite short and simple. You might imagine – as I had – that spells have to be great, long complicated things that go on for pages and for hours. You might think that you always need a bucket of toad spit or a packet of frogs' legs or a dead bat. You probably did for some spells, but not for this one. This one was just a matter of sprinkling a little water and saying the right words.

There were only eight lines altogether. But if you think I'm going to tell you the exact words, I'm not. Not because I don't trust you, I'm sure that you're a very nice person. But not everybody is, and I wouldn't want this sort of knowledge to fall into the wrong hands, or people would be getting swapped all the time.

So in we went for tea. It was a good spread, with all sorts of things on the table. Biscuits, crisps, two kinds of cake and three kinds of sandwiches plus bread and jam. And to drink, there was milk.

'Milk, Meredith?'

'Yes please, Gran.' (She could be nice and polite when she wanted to.)

'Milk, Carly?'

'Thanks.'

The old lady carefully handed us our glasses of milk. To Meredith she gave the tumbler rimmed with ballet dancers. She handed me a tumbler which had little dolphins on it. One of them had a ball balanced on its nose.

'Sandwiches, Carly? Cake? Take whatever you want to. Do help yourself. And Meredith, what about you?'

The clatter of plates. The rattle of cutlery. The sound of dainty eating, of politeness and good manners. Then—

'Gosh, I'm so *thirsty*,' Meredith said. 'It must have been all that running about and climbing. I'm absolutely *parched*.'

She reached out and took her tumbler of milk. I tried not to stare, but I couldn't help myself, and I saw that Grace was watching her, too. Meredith tilted back the glass and swallowed. Down it went. Down went the milk. And with it, down went the sleeping tablets, the powder dissolved in the whiteness, unseen, untasted.

She drank half the glass and licked her lips, just like a cat with a little pink tongue, a cat that had got the cream. Not a suspicion. Not a clue. Not so much as one tiny cloud on her great blue witch's horizon.

Grace was sitting there, a sandwich in her hand, waiting, as I was, for Meredith to finish the milk and for the sleeping draught to do its business.

Not too obvious, I thought. Eat your sandwich. Don't let her suspect. She's not asleep yet.

'Cheers, Carly!'

She still had that half glass to go. Maybe I could encourage her to drink it. I raised my own glass of milk and knocked it gently against hers.

'Cheers, Meredith,' I said. And it was just like we were grown-ups, with glasses of wine, or champagne, toasting each other on some special occasion.

'Bottoms up,' she said. And fitting the action to the word, she tilted the tumbler until its bottom was up and the last of the milk was inside her.

'Bottoms up,' I responded. Not wanting her to get suspicious in any way, I drank my milk down too.

'Ahh!' Meredith said, putting her tumbler down on to the table. 'That was good. Can I have some more, Gran?'

'Yes,' the old lady said. 'Of course.'

She stood up on her rickety old legs and headed for the fridge.

'Biscuit, Meredith?'

I proffered the plate. She reached out.

'Thanks, Carly.'

She took a biscuit. Then suddenly she yawned.

'Oh my!' She covered her hand with her mouth. 'Excuse me. I suddenly feel so—'

Tired? Had she said *tired*? That was funny. I suddenly felt so tired too. It must have been that sleepless night last night. All that worry about things going wrong, that Meredith wouldn't drink the milk, that the witch would have some trick up her sleeve. All that worry, all for nothing. It had all gone splendidly, it had all gone fine. Oh my, I felt so tired, though. I could scarcely keep my eyes open. I felt quite exhausted in fact. I really needed a little sleep. Just a short snooze; forty winks, that was all; just a little rest for a few minutes.

They wouldn't think it rude, would they, my falling asleep at the table like that? But I simply couldn't help myself. My eyes felt so heavy, like great metal doors, like enormous steel shutters closing down. There was nothing I could do to keep them open, or to stop my head lolling forwards and collapsing on to my arms folded in front of me on the table.

I'd be all right. Just as soon as I'd had a little snooze. That was all I needed. Just a snooze. Then everything would be right as rain . . . as rain . . . as rain . . .

That was the last thing I remembered. There was no more until I woke up. That was the very last image I recollected: the picture of Meredith and of Grace, both looking at each other. Looking at me, and then looking at each other, and grinning, smiling, but not in a nice way. Not nice smiles. Not nice smiles at all. Grim, hard, vicious, malevolent smiles. The way the devil must smile when he catches a soul and drags it down to hell.

And that was all I can recall. The next thing was sleep, a long, long tunnel of deep, deep sleep. A tunnel that led to other tunnels. A tunnel like a sewer under a great city. And somewhere, behind a wall, there were voices, faraway voices, the sound of voices singing, or maybe chanting, reciting a poem, reading a spell. Then there were scurrying and scratching noises, like the gnawing of rats from behind a skirting board, or from under a floor.

And that was all I remembered.

Until I woke up.

And when I awoke . . .

. . . I wasn't me any more.

11

Awake

Then I woke up and it was all a dream.

I think that everybody writes that once. Like when you do some fantastic story for your English homework, and it's the best story you've ever written, with ten out of ten looking straight back at you, if only you can work out how to end it. (And without having to do another page.) And then it comes to you.

I woke up and it was all a dream.

But sometimes when you wake up, it's to find that it wasn't all a dream at all. It's to find that the reality you have woken up to is nothing but a living nightmare.

I woke up – the slow way. Not wide awake all at once. More the slow, one piece at a time waking, that 'Who-am-I? Where-am-I? What-am-I-doing-here?' waking that you sometimes get in unfamiliar places, on sleep-overs in friends' houses, or on your holidays.

This pillow's hard! That's the first thing I remember, feeling that hard pillow under my head like a lump of solid wood. Then I moved my head a little, maybe slurped a bit, the way you do when you find you've been asleep with your mouth open.

Then I opened my eyes.

They didn't feel right. There was something wrong

with them. They just didn't feel like my eyes any more. Then other things too. The feel of my mouth. It's amazing all the things you come to accept and to take for granted. The feel and taste of your own mouth, the way the air comes through your nostrils, the shape of your nose, the way you blink, the way you sit or swallow or sigh.

None of it was me.

I wasn't in a bed either. I wasn't lying down at all. I was sitting on a chair, slumped over something. Yes, a table. I looked closely. Some things were in focus, others weren't. I seemed to be looking through something, small windows, tiny windows, which made the world sharp or left it blurred.

Yes, a table. A kitchen table. That was where I was. I'd been asleep on a kitchen table, my head half cradled in my arms.

My arms? *Were* those my arms? They seemed to have grown. I felt so groggy too. Maybe I'd been telling lies and my arms had grown, just like Pinnochio's nose. Only *what* lies? And how could telling lies make your arms grow?

Something else as well. A smell. Yes, a smell. Isn't it funny how we all have a smell, but we don't notice it until it changes, or something changes it.

I didn't even smell like me. I used to have a young smell. I used to smell of fresh air and a bath every evening. My hair smelt of shampoo and the rest of me of soap. Sometimes, after we'd been swimming, I might smell of chlorine a bit. But even that was a fresh, clean, pungent sort of smell. This was different.

It wasn't a nasty smell. It was just different.

It was a lavender smell; a woolly hat, baggy old

144

coat smell; it was a smell of old clothes – clean, but old just the same, clothes which had had all the life and shape and newness washed out of them a long time ago.

> Lavender blue, Dilly-Dilly, Lavender green
> When you are King, Dilly-Dilly,
> I shall be Queen.

Why had I thought of that? Why were fragments of old rhymes and flashes of pictures and scenery I was sure I had never looked on coming into my mind? They stayed only briefly, and then they were gone. Memories too, of things I'd never done, places I'd never been to. Yet they weren't my imagination. They were memories, *real* memories. Don't ask me how I knew that, but I knew.

They scuttled away. It was like letting the light into a darkened room. A smelly old beach hut. That's what it was. All full of crabs and insects, crawling on the floor. Insect memories. Then the door was opened and the light came in – that must have been me, waking up and opening my eyes and yawning. As soon as the light came in, the cockroach memories were startled and frightened and they vanished away. They didn't like the light. They were gone. They couldn't live where there was sunlight. They were memories that lived in darkness and gloom. Witch memories, yes, witch memories, of days of long ago, of wickedness and evil, malice and venom. Black cat memories. Tiptoeing down dark alleyways and jumping over the dustbin lids.

I stretched. Tried to stretch. But the stretch

wouldn't come. What was wrong? This wasn't my normal stretch. I was like a rubber band that had got old and had dried out, which had grown brittle and cracked, like sun-baked riverbank mud, or icing on a cake which should have been eaten long ago.

No real stretch at all. I tried again, but no stretch would come. All the springiness had gone from me. I didn't even feel like a child any more. Not supple and new, and able to twist and turn in all directions.

I felt like a bundle of sticks. Yes. Dry sticks all tied together with a loop of string. And I was wearing old clothes that must have come from a jumble sale. Maybe I belonged to a farmer now, that was it. I'd been put to work as a scarecrow. That would explain why I felt as dry as a bundle of sticks, why my fingers felt like twigs, and my arms and legs like the thin, shrivelled branches of a gnarled and ancient tree.

I was a scarecrow girl. It all made sense now. I was a scarecrow.

But if I was a scarecrow, where was the field? Where were the crows to scare?

I listened. If I listened hard I should hear them.

Yes, there they were – 'Caw, caw!' 'Caw, caw!'

There were the crows. Just over there. Crows and rooks. On the other side of the table.

'Caw, caw,' they went. 'Caw, caw!' Almost as if they were laughing, jeering at me. Two crows laughing. You could write a poem about that.

But wait a minute. That wasn't right either. Crows and scarecrows at the table. The kitchen table? No, that was wrong. You didn't get that. Crows and scarecrows were outside things, out in the fields, farmers' things. They weren't in-the-kitchen things.

146

But 'Caw, caw!' – that's what they were saying.

Or were they?

No they weren't. Maybe not after all.

I raised my head. Oh, my poor old head. How long had I been there? I felt I'd been asleep a long time. Didn't feel any better for it, though. Worse, if anything.

Oh, my.

Yawning now. But something wrong there, too. My teeth. Loose. All joined together in two bits, but loose too. Not attached to my mouth properly. Almost like in sets. Two sets. Top set, bottom set. Rattled a bit. Went click, click, click.

'Caw, caw, caw!' again. Laughing at the click, click, click.

Not crows at all. I could see that now. Peering through the little windows as I straightened up my head.

My head, though. So groggy still, and full of sleep. Need to open a window and let some fresh air into my groggy old head. Open one of my little windows.

Rub my eyes.

No. Can't. Windows in the way. Windows? Glasses, of course. That's what they were.

When had I started wearing glasses? When had Mum got me glasses? I remember going to the optician's to get my eyes tested, but I don't remember the glasses . . .

I was all right.

I thought.

Look, though. What was this? What was I looking at here, through the glasses. Someone's hands. But look at them. Such poor, old hands. So lined and

147

wrinkled and crooked. And yet when I said *Move!* to them – they moved.

But that couldn't be right.

Try an experiment.

Right finger move!

It moved. Not very well, though. Hurt a bit, too. Stiff and sore. Whose finger was it? Why did it hurt like that? How come *I* could move it? How come I could feel somebody else's aches and pains?

'Caw, caw, caw!'

What *was* that noise? What was that irritating, dreadful noise? Like those things at the zoo. The ones that laughed, seeming to mock you; even in captivity they were full of derision. Hyenas. Was that it? Hyenas? But they weren't birds. Maybe I was thinking of kookaburras. Maybe something else. Parrots? Mynah birds?

'Caw, caw, caw! Who's Carly now!'

What was that? They spoke? Crows didn't speak, nor hyenas.

I could see them better now. Swimming into focus. Funny how things could swim into focus. Just like the world was water and everything swam in it – in and out of focus.

Girls. There were two girls. Looking at me. Smiling. No. Not smiling. Smiling was nice. This wasn't nice. Grinning. Grimacing. Something else in those expressions too – cunning, malice, triumph, hatred, evil.

'Caw, caw! Ha, ha! Look at the old lady! Who's Carly now!'

Who's Carly? What did they mean? *I* was Carly. Everyone knew that. Mum and Dad and everyone at

148

school, and the teachers and the dentist and the neighbours and, well, everyone, really, and Meredith, and Grace, and—

Meredith. It was coming back to me now. Me and Meredith and Grace and the spell and the sleeping pills and drinking the milk and Meredith falling asleep and—

No. I didn't recollect that exactly. Not seeing her fall asleep. It seemed more that I had fallen asleep.

Me? Asleep? Then when about the spell? Who had said the spell? To swap the souls around. To put Meredith back into her rightful body. Who said the spell? I was supposed to say it. But I didn't say anything. I just – fell asleep.

'Caw, caw, caw! Look at the old ratbag! Who's the old ratbag now!'

How nasty. What a nasty thing to say. What a nasty girl. What nasty girls. Yes. There were two of them. I could see them both quite clearly, through the little windows of the glasses balanced on my nose.

That was an odd feeling too, the sensation of glasses balanced on your nose. They pinched just a little, and I could feel the ends of the frame, folded around the tops of my ears. I remembered that from holidays, when you had to put your sunglasses on. That was the only time I'd ever worn glasses. The only time at all.

'Silly old ratbag. Stupid old bat!'

Who were they talking to? They needed to learn a few manners, those girls. Teach them a few manners, somebody should. You should be a bit politer to old people, my mum said. We all grow old and nobody can help it, and old people have been through lots and lots sometimes. Maybe more happiness and sadness than you could ever imagine. And they were children once, too. And one day you'll be old yourself. My mum says.

'Caw, caw!'

Such rude girls.

But who *were* those girls? Sitting there at the other end of the table.

Meredith. That was one. Meredith. Was it the *real* Meredith, now? Not the witch any more? Had everything been sorted out while I was asleep? Was everything OK? Could we all go home now and live happily ever after, just like in the fairy tales and when the story's over?

Could we?

Only wait. Who was that other girl? The one next to Meredith. The one sticking her tongue out at me, and putting her thumb to her nose and waggling her fingers and going, 'Na, na, nee, na, na – who's a dozy old bat!'

That one. Now what? Putting her thumbs up by her ears now, waggling the fingers of both hands.

> 'Granny, Granny, Carly is a granny.
> She's as old as ice is cold,
> Carly is a granny.'

Who was that rude girl? I knew her from somewhere. Only where was it, now? I'd seen that face before. Only not quite looking like that. Usually in more of a – well, a mirror image. Not exactly straight on. Except – yes – in photographs. I'd seen it in photographs. It was someone I knew. I'd seen her loads of times. I used to see her everywhere, every day, in the bathroom mirror in the morning, reflected in windows and glass. I'd seen that face looking long and thin at funfairs, in the hall of mirrors, then suddenly it would be squat and fat, and then it would be normal again.

It was *me*. I was looking at myself. I was watching myself stick my tongue out at me, I was listening to my own voice mock me and laugh at me.

But how? How could there be two of me? One there, and one here? How could I be sitting in two different chairs at once, at opposite ends of the table?

How could—?

Then it all made sense. So swiftly and suddenly. Like falling into freezing cold water. My heart was full of ice, and I felt fear to the pit of my stomach.

Oh no, oh no, oh, no, no, no! I looked at my hands again. At the swollen knuckles, the stiff joints, the thin, wrinkled, parchment skin. The aches, the pains, the glasses, the teeth, the musty smell, the stretch that wouldn't come. I wasn't in me any more. I was somewhere else. I wasn't young. I was a thousand, a million, a trillion billion and one years old. I was older than anyone, older than the stars. I was old, old, old.

I was in the old woman's body. Not Meredith, not Grace, not anyone else. *Me*. Me, me, me! Something had gone wrong. Something had happened. Some terrible evil, awful trick. I looked down at myself, at my old, slow, dried-up, shrivelled self, dressed in the old, shapeless clothes.

'Mum!' I cried. 'Mum, Mum, Mum! Dad! Mum!

151

Help me, help me! Somebody help me! Somebody help me! *Please!'*

But 'Caw, caw, caw!' the crows went on cackling. The two great girl-shaped crows at the other end of the table just went on cackling more and more, and louder and louder, almost as though they were preparing to fly somewhere, getting ready for take-off, flapping big, invisible wings.

'Caw, caw, caw! Carly's a fogey! Carly's a dozy old fogey! Caw, caw caw!'

Then everything spun around me. I was in the centre of a whirlpool, a tornado; everything spun around me, then I started spinning too. Spinning so fast that I could no longer keep my head upright or my eyes open. And I pitched forwards and my head went *Crack!* upon the table.

I passed out in a dead faint.

Then I slept. I wanted to sleep for ever and never to wake. That would be the best thing. That would be an end to the nightmare of being awake. To sleep for ever in a dreamless sleep. Maybe that was what death was. That wasn't so bad. Not when living was suddenly so wretched, so horrible . . .

So I slept. Maybe it was only for a few moments, maybe for longer, maybe for hours. Maybe.

But then my worst nightmare happened.

I woke up again.

12

Abandoned

The light had changed. It was a later light. When you don't have a watch on you, or a clock to see, you can often tell the time by the quality of light. You just need to know what season you're in, and then you can judge it.

It was growing darker, and it was autumn. That must have made it six, or even seven. My head spun like a top as I tried to make sense of it all.

Lies within lies – they tumbled and turned, like wheels within wheels, layers within layers. Peel one back and there's another still, and then another under that. Where was the truth? How did I find it? How many lies had they told me to win my confidence? Was it true about Meredith and the orphanage? Yes, maybe, probably, perhaps. About the astral projection then, and flying through the night? Maybe, I supposed. It was vague and unclear, what powers they had and what powers they didn't; which ones had faded with age and which ones were still full and strong. They had needed me to be drugged and unconscious, that was plain enough, to get their spell to work, otherwise . . .

The lies of witches were like thin ice on a deep river. From a distance everything seemed fine. Then

153

out you went, further out, and gradually put your full weight and trust on the fragile structure beneath you. And before you knew it, you had broken through, and were drowning in the freezing water.

I rubbed my eyes, the way old people do, as if their eyes are full of memories that just won't go away. I noticed my hands had patterns on them, made by all the criss-crossing wrinkles.

I tried to think.

I ought to be getting home. Mum would be wondering where I was. The phone would ring soon. It would be her, or Dad, asking Meredith's granny if I needed picking up, or if they would be walking me home.

Home. Yes. I had to get home. Get home and explain to Mum and Dad what had happened. About me being an old lady now. They'd put it right, they'd understand. Dad was a solicitor. He could sort it out. He could take them to court. Or something. *Something*. And Mum had trained as a nurse. She had gone back to it recently. Part-time anyway. She could do something. She'd been a casualty department nurse at the hospital – she was used to dealing with emergencies.

And this definitely was an emergency. A lights-flashing, sirens-blaring, fire, police and ambulance emergency, if ever there was one.

I was alone in the kitchen. The two girls had gone. Meredith and – what did I call her? Not 'Carly', because that was me. I might be in this old body, but I was still me, still young, still Carly.

Meredith and my body then. Where had they gone? I stood up shakily, rubbing my head where it had whacked against the table. I walked unsteadily to the sink to get a glass of water. The remains of the tea were still on the table. A plate with a half a cake on it; some sandwiches; two empty glasses of milk.

I drank the cold water thirstily, gulping it down. I shuddered. It felt cold and creepy to be inside such an old body. I felt as if I'd turned into a great lizard.

Footsteps. They were back. Both of them. Wearing coats now, outdoor coats. As if off out somewhere, ready to go.

Ready to go *where*?

But where was my coat? That old lady's coat? A coat to fit me. I had to get home. I told them so.

'I have to get home,' I said. 'Or my mum will be worried.'

'Caw, caw, caw!' They started to cackle again. I wished they wouldn't do that.

'*My mum will be worried,*' Meredith said, imitating the sound of the frail voice I now had. 'She thinks her mum will be worried,' she jeered. 'Well, let me tell you something,' she said. 'It's not you she'll be worried about, because you're just an old woman now. It's this young lady she'll be worried about. This Carly. The one with your body. Not you.'

I sat down. I felt dizzy again.

'How—' I began. 'Why—?'

Meredith looked at the other girl – I shall have to call her Carly. It'll get too confusing otherwise. I know she isn't really, but there's no other way to talk about her, for the moment.

'Shall we tell her?' Meredith asked. 'Shall we tell her how we did it? Before we go?'

Carly shrugged and gave a little sneer.

'Why not?' she said. 'If it doesn't take too long. I have to get home soon, remember – or *my mum will be wondering.*'

And she laughed her nasty little laugh.

'OK,' Meredith said. 'It's like this. We're sisters. The two of us. Both witches and both as old as the hills. We're as old as the hills before they were hills. We're as old as the valleys and the streams, as old as the sea. We've seen more things than you've ever dreamed of and lived longer than you'll ever know. We're immortal, you might say. But not in the way that people generally imagine. Our bodies grow old and wear out, same as anyone's. But when they do, that's the time to jump ship and to get yourself a new one.

'Now when it's time for us to find new bodies, we try to do it together, at the same time. But it's not always possible. Sometimes we can only find one. Sometimes we get lucky and find a matching pair. Sometimes it's boys, sometimes it's girls. Last time, it was sisters. But we have to be careful whose body we steal. We usually like to find an orphan, or somebody like that without any family, who nobody's going to miss. We trick them with promises – it's ever so simple. You wouldn't believe how hungry some girls and boys are for love. You only have to promise them a home and a little bit of affection, and they'll trust you implicitly, won't they, my dear?'

She looked at Carly, who had cut herself a piece of cake and was busy chewing it.

'Implicitly, my dear sister,' she said. 'Implicitly and stupidly, but completely. The poor love-starved mites. Such a shame – poor things.'

'But it would be an even bigger shame if *we* had to stay old and get even older and then die,' Meredith added.

'That,' Carly nodded, 'would be such a great and disastrous shame that we couldn't possibly let it happen.'

'No,' Meredith said. 'And we don't. So as I say, sometimes we find two bodies to steal together – twins or something like that. Other occasions we have to steal one body at a time.'

'We take it in turns to be the first when that happens,' Carly explained.

'Now the clever bit though,' Meredith said, 'is that as soon as we have one body, we can use it as bait to steal the other.'

'Which is just what we did with *you*, my dear Carly,' Carly smirked.

I nearly had to pinch myself. It all felt so unreal. To be sitting there listening to my own body talk to me, to look at my own hair, my own freckles and podgy bits, to hear my own voice, to hear it call me Carly.

'Yes, I'm afraid that we took you in from the word go.'

'But the story,' I said, in my old, trembling, rather reedy voice. 'About Meredith and the orphanage—'

'Oh, that part was true enough. But what I didn't tell you was that Meredith was looked after not by *one* old lady, but by *two*. By Grace and—'

'And by her sister Briony,' Carly said. 'And I'm Grace!'

'And I'm really Briony,' Meredith grinned.

'But the real Meredith – what became of her?'

'What do you think?' Meredith said. 'Once we had her body, we didn't have any use for her any more—'

'You *killed* her?!' I croaked, suddenly more terrified than ever. Was that what they were going to do to me? To kill me? It was bad enough to be so old. But it was better than being dead. I still had hope, maybe even a chance—

'Killed her?' Meredith said indignantly. 'Certainly not! What do you take us for? We're not uncivilized, you know. We do have some standards. No. We just got rid of her.'

'Stuck her in an old folks' home, as a matter of fact,' Carly said. 'Not all that far from here. She was getting a bit old and dribbly. You don't really want that sort of thing around the place. It can put you off your dinner.'

'And besides,' Meredith pointed out, 'why would we *need* to kill her? She'll be dead soon anyway, an old codger like that.'

'Dicky ticker,' Carly nodded.

'Or maybe a stroke.'

'Lose her marbles.'

'Memory going.'

'No life, no life at all.'

'No *quality* of life.'

'None,' Meredith agreed. 'Not worth living.'

'Not like being young.'

'Best put out to grass.'

'Best kept out of sight.'

'Best locked away in a home somewhere.'

'With like-minded people of her own age.'

'Or no-minded people.'

'But people she'd have something in common with.'

'Like being old and smelly.'

'And she can sit in front of the TV all day.'

'And suck her teeth.'

'Or someone else's teeth – these mix-ups can happen.'

'And peer out of the window through her glasses.'

'Big, thick glasses. Like cola bottles.'

'Not much of a life.'

'Not much at all. Too bad. What a shame. Never even was a girl, really.'

'Never got a chance to grow up, or fall in love.'

'Never had a childhood.'

'But not to worry. She's being put to good use. Her body's not being wasted. It's fallen into safe hands. It's with someone who'll look after it, just as if it were their own – me!'

'And me!'

'Caw, caw caw!'

And the two witches danced around the room, like models on a catwalk, showing off this season's latest styles. 'Over here,' they seemed to be saying, 'there's the tall and willowy look, while here is the red-haired look with freckles and podgy bits.'

'You put the real Meredith into a home?' I said. 'That poor girl, that orphan? There really was an orphan called Meredith?'

'Of course. And this is her body, like I said. But we needed another body – your body. It's very easy, you see, once you've got hold of one body, to get another. You can trick people so easily. They don't suspect young people of being witches. And certainly not somebody who looks like this – so tall and willowy.'

'That's right,' Carly said, washing her cake down with a swig of milk straight from the bottle. 'So we just switched the glasses round and gave you the milk with the sleeping powder in it. Then once you'd nodded off, it was a simple matter of saying the spell. The joke is, you don't even need to be a witch to make it work. Some spells you need fully-fledged witch's powers for, but other spells, anyone can do, if they have the right formula and the right secret words.'

'That's right,' Meredith grinned, 'And now here we are. And there *you* are. Sorry you've got to be old so soon. Still, never mind, it won't last for ever. Look on the bright side, you might be dead in a year or two. Maybe even in a couple of months, if you get lucky. So you won't be stuck in that old prison of a body for too long.'

They both headed for the door.

'But where are you *going*?' I said. 'What are you going to *do*? You can't just leave me like this. You can't. My mum, my dad – my stick insects!'

They laughed again. I don't know why I'd said that about the stick insects. It just came out.

'Stick insects! She's worried about her stick insects! Look at yourself – you *are* a stick insect. An old, skinny, wizened, crotchety, old stick insect. All dried up and scaly. That's *you*!'

I wanted to cry. But I was beyond it now. I was too upset to cry.

'But *why*!' I demanded. '*Why*! Why did you tell me all those lies? Why did you ask me to help you? Why did you trick me and deceive me like that? Why, why, *why*?'

Meredith looked at me, cold and hard.

'Because we could, Carly. Because you were trusting and all too ready to help someone who pretended to be in need. Because you were kind. Because we could see that you were a little bit lonely and wanted a friend and a sister. Because you were easy to trick.'

Sister? A sister. Wait a minute. No. No. It couldn't be. That wasn't possible too, was it? They hadn't planned that part as well?

'But wait – my mum and dad – going to see them, pretending to be worried that Meredith wouldn't have a home if anything should happen to the old lady, getting them to agree that Meredith could move in – into my home, and be my sister—'

Meredith gave her thin smile.

'That's right, Carly. You've finally got it. It takes you a long time to twig on, but you get there in the end. We're going to move into your house. And your parents will never know. And we're going to be such well-behaved and lovely little girls, aren't we, sister?'

'Oh, yes,' the other one simpered, ' oh, yes we are.'

'And we'll sit tight and bide our time and be such perfect children that no one will ever suspect—'

'But when we've been in these bodies long enough—'

'And our full witches' powers return to us—'

'We'll start to take over. And maybe tell them the truth.'

'Tell them that their own dear, darling, little daughter is stuck in an old woman's body—'

'In some old folk's home, somewhere.'

'But they won't be able to do anything about it.'

'Because by then she might already be dead.'

'And even if she isn't, they still won't be able to do anything. And if they try, we'll do something unpleasant to them. Like turn them both into worms—'

'And then step on them. Or pour salt on them, until they turn inside out!'

They opened the door.

'So, bye, Carly. Thanks for the body. It wouldn't have been my first choice. But red hair and freckles can be quite attractive in their own way. And I'm sure that as I get older, the podgy bits will wear off. So thanks. And bye then.'

'But you can't just *go*!' I screamed. I didn't mean it to come out as a scream, it just did. 'You can't just move into my house. My mum and dad won't just let Meredith move in! They'll ask questions. They'll want to know about me. About what I'm doing.'

Meredith turned in the doorway and looked back at me.

'I'm afraid, old woman,' she said, 'that you are no longer fit to look after me. I think that will soon become plain to everyone. Goodbye.'

'Goodbye, Carly,' Carly said. 'Enjoy your life – what's left of it. And remember, every day is a gift to be treasured. So even if you can't do cartwheels any more, you could always take up knitting. Bye.'

And they were gone.

The telephone rang. After a while I stood up to answer it. I felt so old and stiff and slow, and in so much pain. I reached out to pick up the receiver, but the ringing stopped.

I dialled 1471. A voice told me which number the

162

caller had dialled from. I recognized it immediately. It was ours. It must have been my mum ringing, wondering when I was coming home.

I took the phone. I could ring her straight back, right now. I could warn her, explain, tell her about the two witches who were on their way, that both of them were wolves in sheeps' clothing. And that one of the sheep was me.

But no. That wouldn't work. Just to talk to her in my old lady's voice. She'd just think I was Grace, she wouldn't understand. I had to go there. She had to see me in person. She'd know then, from my eyes, from something in me. She'd know me, she would. She was my mum. She'd know it was really me, trapped in an old woman's body, even if nobody else could. She'd believe me, she'd help me. My mum and dad, they'd believe me, they'd know. Blood was thick, wasn't it, thicker than water. Parents knew their own children. They'd help me to be myself again. They would, they would.

I put on my old lady's coat. It was cold out. I had to keep warm. I had to be careful. I couldn't take chances. I was an old lady now.

There was a walking stick by the door. I hesitated, then decided to take it. Better safe than sorry. I didn't want to stumble or trip on the kerb and break my hip. Things like that could take for ever to heal, when you were old. And to think that only a few short hours ago I had been young and lithe and—

The door slammed behind me. I hurried on down the path. I hurried, but made slow progress. My corns hurt, and my bunions, and how those shoes pinched, just there, around the toes. My knees seemed to

163

creak, and my elbow ached when I leaned on the stick.

But on I went. Head down, one foot after the other, head bowed but determined. I had to get there before them. No. That was impossible. I could never overtake them, they were far too fast, they were two young girls. Why, they could *run*! But maybe I could run, too? Ouch! No. I couldn't. Must be more careful, nearly fell that time. Nice and steady now, that's the way.

On I went, with my old lady walk and my old lady paces. I wouldn't get there before them, but I had to get home as soon as I could, before the witches were able to poison the minds of the two people who I was certain loved me. My mum and my dad.

They'd taken my body, but they couldn't take my home. Not my family. Not my mum and dad. They couldn't do that. They'd believe me. They'd love me still and for ever, even if I was an old lady now.

Mum and Dad.

They were my only hope. They'd know it was really me. Wouldn't they?

13

Home

The world had changed. The puddles weren't things I could jump over any more. A skip, a quick hop would have done it before. But now I had to make my slow way around them, fearful that I might trip, or stumble, or fall, then lie there like a turtle and not be able to get up again.

The night was getting darker. Yellow street lights were coming on.

Footsteps!

Was that a mugger? Creeping up behind me, to snatch an old lady's handbag.

I put on a turn of speed.

Did I say speed? Well, you know what I mean. Old lady speed. Pitter-patter speed, little footstep speed, accompanied by the tip-tap rattle of a walking stick.

The footsteps passed. It was no one. Well, it was someone, but no one who wished me harm. My house wasn't far away, but it was taking so long to get there. It was so . . . *inconvenient* having to be old. Such a nuisance. It so slowed you down.

At last I turned the corner into our street. There was our house, halfway along. Everything was as it should be. The lights were on in the living-room, the car was in the drive. It all looked cosy and warm and comfortable, just like going home should.

I pushed open the gate and walked up the path towards the front door, pausing to look into the living-room, to see if the two witches were there.

They were. Both of them. Sitting and watching the television. My mum was at the window, reaching up to draw the curtains, as she must have done hundreds of times. It seemed like something eternal. It was ordinary, solid, reassuring. Nothing could go really wrong, everything could be put right and be fixed. As long as my mum was there, doing what she always did, at exactly the right time. She'd fix it. She was good at fixing things. It was going to be OK.

She squinted out at me, peering into the darkness, as I reached to ring the doorbell.

'I'll go. It's probably someone to collect the charity envelope.'

It was my dad's voice, calling faintly from the kitchen, or maybe from his study.

I rang the doorbell again, impatient, anxious. His voice grew louder.

'Coming, coming! Hold on!'

My dad. It was him. He'd soon know, he'd understand, he'd soon get rid of those girls.

There they were again. A chink of light and two faces looking out at me through a gap in the curtains. Smug and sure, nasty little faces. Triumphant, victorious, gloating.

'Good evening.' The door opened, Dad was there, a charity envelope with lumpy money in it in his hand, just sticking the top of the envelope down. 'I expect you've come to collect the—'

'Dad—'

He looked puzzled. He reached out and turned on the outside light to be able to see me better.

'I'm sorry?'

'It's me – it's *me* – *Carly*!'

'I'm sorry? You wanted Carly? She's in the front room actually, I think, with a friend. Can I ask who's—'

Mum appeared behind him in the hall, her arms full of washing.

'Mum!'

She stopped, stared, wondering who it was.

'It's me! It's me!'

She edged forwards.

'Shelley – do you know this lady?'

Mum stopped by the door, saw who it was and seemed relieved. She smiled with recognition.

'Grace!' Then she turned to my dad. 'It's Meredith's granny.' Then to me. 'They're both in the living-room. Come in. Meredith said you'd be round.'

'But *Mum*—'

She seemed to freeze. She glanced at Dad, he shot a look back at her, a troubled, wary look, as if someone was behaving strangely.

But they knew it was me, didn't they? They could tell it was me.

'Mum, it's *me*, Carly. It's me, your little girl.'

She recoiled, took a step backwards. Why was she walking away from me like that? Why didn't she put her arms around me and give me a cuddle like she usually did when I'd just come home?

'Mum—'

167

She turned to Dad, talking like a grown-up, the way they do when there's trouble – the big serious kind.

'John—'

'It's all right. Probably just a turn – better get a chair, maybe . . .'

'Yes, right.'

Mum hurried to bring a chair from the kitchen.

'Come in, won't you, Grace,' Dad said as she went to fetch it. 'Are you OK? You look a little pale? Is everything all right?'

I was starting to cry. Big, globby tears came to my eyes and there was nothing I could do to stop them spilling over. I stepped into the hall, reaching out with my arms.

'Dad,' I said, and I was sobbing now, fit to drown the carpet. 'Dad, it's me, Carly. They've stolen me, stolen my body. Meredith and her sister. They're witches, you see, both witches. And that's what they do, so they can live for ever. They take one body and then another. And when it's old and done and worn out, they don't care, they just go and steal another one. They did it to Meredith and now they've done it to me. They stole her body and put her in an old folks' home. And it's not fair, not fair. Please, Dad, please help me, please.'

He backed away. As if he had seen something horrible, something repulsive and vile.

'Dad, Dad, it's me, Carly! It's me! Your little girl!'

I wanted a cuddle. Why wouldn't he take me in his arms and give me a cuddle? Just like we always did. All the time, loads of times. Swing me round like he used to, round and round until I screamed for him to stop, though I wanted it go to on really, and when he finally did stop, I'd only ask him to do it again.

'Dad, it's Carly, your daughter, your little girl – Carly – it's *me*!'

He was still backing away. He was looking at me as if I were mad. Mad and uncontrolled and disturbed.

'Dad! It's true! I can see you don't believe me, but it's true. They've stolen my body, my youth, my life. She's pretending to be me. But *I'm* me. I know I don't look like me but it is me, Dad. Ask me a question, any question, I'll be able to answer it, but she won't. Ask me the name of the cat, Aunty Barbara's name, the colour of the wallpaper in my room, how much I've got saved up in my savings account. I know, Dad, to the nearest penny. Dad . . . Dad . . . ?'

He didn't speak. Just stood there. Mum was back now with the chair from the kitchen. Dad looked at her.

'Shelley, did you—?'

'I heard, yes. Every word.' She placed the seat squarely in the middle of the hall. 'Grace, here. Please sit down.'

'No, I'm all right,' I said. 'I don't need to sit down! All I need is for someone to *believe* me!'

But they weren't looking at me, or even listening. They were looking at each other, talking around me and above my head, as if I wasn't really there.

'What do you think it is?'

'Minor stroke, maybe.'

'Could be. You don't think it might be the onset of dementia?'

'I hope not. I hope not, for Meredith's sake.'

'Mum! Dad! *Listen*!'

'It's often how it starts, though. Not knowing who people are. Thinking someone in the present is really a figure from the past.'

'Mum! Dad! Listen to me! It's me in here. It's Carly. It is. Carly! I've been *stolen*.'

'Hear that? She thinks she's Carly.'

'Yes. Why would she think that?'

'Odd, isn't it? You'd think she'd think she was Meredith if she was going to think she was anyone.'

'So unpredictable, though.'

'What'll we do?'

'Who's her doctor?'

'I don't know.'

'Better call someone. I'll do it. You'd better talk to Meredith.'

'*Meredith!*'

The faces were there at the living-room door, peering out, all innocence, all eager to help and anxious to please – and under it all, pure evil.

'Yes, Mrs Taylor?'

'Your gran's here. But she doesn't seem very well. Do you know the name of her doctor?'

'No, I'm afraid not, Mrs Taylor,' Meredith simpered, in her butter-wouldn't-melt tones. 'Sorry.' And then she had the nerve to come right up to me and to look concerned, to put her hand on my forehead to feel if it was hot, as if she cared and was worried about me.

'Aren't you feeling well, Gran?' she said. 'Are you feeling a bit under the weather?'

'Get your hands off me, you nasty witch!' I

170

screamed, and struck out at her, knocking her hands away.

Mum and Dad stared at me, more sure than ever that I'd had a stroke or lost my marbles.

Meredith backed away. Then you know what she did? You know what she had the nerve to do? She pretended to *cry*. She actually pretended to *cry*!

'Oh, Granny,' she wailed. 'Why did you hit me? I was only asking how you were. I was only trying to help.'

'Ahhhhh! Why you—' I let out another angry scream. A really terrifying one this time. And before I knew it, I had raised my walking stick up in the air, and was just taking aim when a strong hand stopped me. It held me by the wrist.

'I think that'll do now, Grace.' It was my dad's voice. He very gently took away the walking stick. 'There's no need for that now.' He put the stick down under the umbrella stand. 'Nothing to worry about at all. You've just had a bit of a turn, that's all. You're not your usual self.'

'Of course I'm not my usual self!' I snapped. 'How could I be my usual self when I'm in someone else's body! I'm a girl. Not an old fogey! Don't be so stupid, Dad! Honestly!'

Mum and Dad both thought I was definitely mad now. Eyeballs were turning to the ceiling.

'Meredith can't possibly go back home with her tonight,' Mum whispered.

'She'd better stay with us,' Dad said.

'What?!' I began. 'No! You musn't! That's exactly what they *want*. They want to take you over. Like maggots in an apple. Like head lice – parasites! They want to live off you! They just need you to look after them for a while. So no one will ask any questions or get suspicious. Just so they can be safe while they grow up. But as soon as they have all their powers back, they'll finish you off too!'

But nobody was listening. Once people have decided that everything you say is lies, they switch off, they don't listen any more, they probably don't even hear. You're completely dismissed.

'Now we're just going to make one or two phone calls, Grace,' my dad was saying, 'and while we're waiting, perhaps you'd like a nice cup of tea.'

'Tea!' I yelled. 'I don't want tea! I don't drink tea, Dad, you know that. I have milk and hot chocolate and orange juice. I don't have cups of *tea*. I hate tea. And beer – I hate that, too. I tried some of yours once, remember, and had to spit it out into the sink. Remember Dad, remember? Believe me now?'

A cloud of uncertainty crossed his gaze. For a moment Mum looked unsure too. The glanced at each other, as though to say, 'What do *you* think?'

'But – but that must be such a common memory,' Dad said to Mum. 'So many children must have done that. She must have done it when she was a girl, tasted her own father's beer and not liked it and spat it out – she's just getting confused, mixing up the present and the past.'

'I'm not confused!' I shrieked in my old lady's croak. 'It's you! Dad, how can you be so blinkered. I used to think you were clever and intelligent. How can you be so – thick!'

He headed for the kitchen.

'I'd better make that phone call,' he said.

'Yes,' Mum nodded. 'And tell them it's urgent. And maybe try to get hold of Social Services as well. They must have an out-of-hours emergency number.'

'Right,' he said. And he went.

Mum turned to me.

No. Not to *me*. I mean the other me. She turned to Carly. To what used to be me. To what she thought was me. To the witch in my body.

'Carly, I think that this must be all rather upsetting for Meredith. Would you maybe like to take her up to your room for a while?'

But '*My* room!' I yelled. 'It's *my* room, not *hers!*' And I said it so venomously that my false teeth nearly fell out, and I had to struggle to get them back in.

They ignored me. The way people on trains ignore someone who is drunk and behaving badly. They pretend they can't see him, and the more he goes on ranting, the more invisible he becomes.

'If you could just take Meredith up to your room for a while, Carly, just until we get things sorted out. Maybe play a game or something. I'll come and talk to Meredith in a moment, and explain what's going on. We've just got to sort things out first, OK? It's a little bit of an emergency and we've all got to pull together and then things will be fine. OK?'

'OK, Mum,' 'Carly' said.

'She's not *your* mum, she's *mine!*' I snapped. I sounded petty and childish, and I knew it.

A look of sadness and sorrow crossed Mum's face. I wondered who she was feeling sorry for, for a moment. But then, of course, it was me. The old lady on the chair, whose teeth had nearly fallen out.

The old lady who had lost her mind, who imagined that the woman next to her – who was forty or even fifty years younger than she was – was her own mother.

No wonder she looked sad. My mum was like that. Good and kind, and she hated to see other people suffering. What broke your heart broke hers, too. No wonder she was sad, to see an old lady like me, sitting there chewing on her false teeth, her mind wandering and her thoughts away with the fairies, in some dim and distant memories of a childhood of long ago.

'Mum . . . Mum . . .' I was crying. Nothing would stop the tears. If I cried enough, maybe I would become young again. The tears would make the wrinkles go away, refresh my old, dry parchment skin. I'd do cartwheels and handstands and dangle from the climbing frame by the backs of my knees.

If I cried enough. If I cried enough I'd come back. I'd be me once more, and happy and all the nightmares and the bad things would go away. Maybe a small bowl of tears might do it, or maybe a bucket, or maybe I'd need to fill up the sink. Maybe you could fix anything if you just shed enough tears.

Or maybe they made no difference at all. They didn't even make you feel better.

'Carly, take Meredith with you now. I think Grace is a little upset.'

'OK, Mum. Sure. Come on, Meredith, let's go up to my room. We can go on the computer.'

Off they went. Bumping into each other. Just like sisters who were really getting on well today, like special friends who knew all of each other's secrets and forgave each other everything.

And I had no one. No one to believe me, or to know me, or to understand. And that was the worst thing, to have no one. That was worse than being old.

Up the stairs they went. Side by side. And you'd never have known, never have known. How wicked the innocent can be.

Click. The door of my room closed behind them. Then giggling, the sound of laughter. The laughter of those who have successfully accomplished some wicked plan. Clear, tinkling, happy laughter.

And I so weary, and full of care.

'Mum—'

'How are you now, Grace? Are you feeling better? The girls have gone. I didn't want them to see you like this. I've sent them upstairs.'

'Mum—'

'No. It's Shelley, remember. Shelley? Carly's mum. Carly, in Meredith's class. At school. Meredith's friend. Remember?'

'Mum—'

I reached out to take her hand.

'Mum—'

'We think you've had a stroke, Grace, a minor stroke. And it's affected your memory. And you don't know where you are.'

'I do, Mum. I'm home, Mum. I'm at home.'

'Yes, yes of course. But I'm not your mother, you see, Grace. That's just a trick of memory. I'm actually Shelley, remember? Carly's mum. Carly, remember? Meredith's friend. It won't be long now though. Help's on the way. John's making a few phone calls. He's ringing for the doctor. Are you sure you wouldn't like a cup of tea?'

'Mum, can I hold your hand?'

She started to cry. I was all cried out and dried up. But Mum seemed to have taken up where I'd left off.

She took my hand. Took my hand in both of hers. She knelt down beside me and held my hand.

'OK, Grace. It's OK. I'll hold your hand. Of course I will. It's not much, is it. The least anyone can do. We all grow old, Grace, and need people to be kind. Me too, one day. And Meredith and Carly. Though that's so hard to imagine right now, when they're both so full of life, and so young.'

Her voice was soft and reassuring. I didn't feel so frightened now.

'Mum—'

'Yes, call me that if you want to. If that's what you want. If it helps. Come on now. Let's straighten you out a bit. It's not so bad. Would you like a cushion? Or a softer chair maybe, for your back.'

'Just go on holding my hand, Mum. Don't ever let go of me, will you. Just go on holding my hand. You won't send me away anywhere, will you? You'll let me stay here with you, won't you?'

'We'll see, we'll see . . .'

'I love you, Mum.'

'I – I—'

'Do you love me too? Do you?'

'Of course, I do. Of course.'

'Thank you, Mum. Thank you. When you're old and if you're unhappy, I'm going to hold your hand.

176

Just like you held mine. I won't forget, Mum, I shan't ever forget. You do know I'm Carly, don't you, Mum? You do believe I'm Carly?'

'I—'

'Please, Mum. Say you believe that I'm Carly.'

The kitchen door opened. Dad appeared.

'They're on their way. Fifteen minutes, the doctor thought. He'll examine her and then we can go on from there and decide what's best to do. Where's Meredith?'

'Up in Carly's room.'

'Is she OK – the old lady?'

'She's a bit quieter now.'

'What are you doing?'

'Holding her hand. The poor old thing. She thinks I'm her mum.'

'Poor thing. Poor thing.'

'We all grow old, John.'

'Yes, we all grow old.'

'Dad—'

'Thinks you're her father too.'

'Hold my other hand.'

'Should I?'

'Go on. It'll reassure her till the doctor gets here.'

'OK.'

'Mum and Dad.'

'That's it, love. That's right. Nothing can happen. Everything's fine. Mum and Dad are here now. Mum and Dad are here. They're holding your hand. You'll be OK now till the doctor arrives. Won't be long now, won't be long.'

And from upstairs, from behind a door, the tinkling of laughter, clear as a waterfall in the silence of hills.

Then the sound of a car. Then a sharp, abrupt knocking on the door.

'Must be the doctor. Sounds like he's here.'

And nobody was holding my hand any more.

I wondered what had become of my walking stick.

14

And Home Again

They put me in a home.

I don't know why they call them homes, they're not really homes at all. They may be nice enough places, some of them, but they're anything but homes. Home is where your family is and your memories are. Home isn't a great big, gloomy house with depressing wardrobes and towels with holes in them and rusty bits on the bath. That's just somewhere you put people when you want to get rid of them. Nor is it even a bright, clean, shiny place, with colourful curtains, and vases of flowers. Home is where you want to be, home is where your heart is, and if you don't want to be there, it can't be home at all.

Not that people see it that way, they just think they're being kind. And maybe they are. And if you're old and lonely and want to be looked after and need to be cared for, they're maybe not such bad places at all. But even if they sent you off to live in the Ritz Hotel, it still wouldn't be home. not as far as I was concerned. Not to me.

'Your granny's not well, Meredith,' I heard the doctor say that night after he'd taken a quick look at me and decided I'd lost my marbles. 'She needs proper looking after in a nice friendly place with trained staff who're used to coping with the elderly and confused.'

Confused? I wasn't confused. I was the only one seeing clearly. But you try talking to anyone medical about witches and astral projection and your body being stolen, and see how far you get. They'll be reaching for the tranquillizer gun two seconds after you've started.

Because they *know*, you see. They've got certificates and qualifications and know all sorts of difficult words and the names of every bone in the body. So how could they possibly believe in *witches*. That would be plain silly. They couldn't possibly believe in anything like that. So don't ever start talking about them, that's my advice, or you might end up in a home for the elderly and confused too. Even when you're still young.

Like I was.

I sat in the kitchen, an untasted cup of tea on the table before me. I told them I didn't like tea, but they made me some anyway. They couldn't help it. Grown-ups are like that. When you're very young or very old, grown-ups always think they know what's best for you. They give you what you don't want and say you can't have what you do, as it would be bad for you.

And they call you the same things too – like 'dear' and 'dearie' and 'there's a love'. Sometimes they even say (as Mrs Horrington did), 'There's a good girl,' when they can see quite clearly that you're an old lady.

I don't think you should say, 'There's a good girl,' to old ladies. I don't think that's right.

So there I was, sitting in the kitchen with my cold cup of tea. The doctor had left his case on the table. There were all sorts of gadgets in it, for looking in your eyes and in your ears, and maybe even up your nose, as well. There was a stethoscope for listening to your chest with, and a shiny steel hammer with a rubber bit on the end for tapping your knees.

'The old lady's reflexes seem all right,' he said, after he'd asked me to cross one leg over the other and he'd given my knee a tap. As soon as he did my leg shot out and I accidentally kicked him. He dropped his hammer under the table and Dad went and got it back.

'Physically, she seems in reasonable health – for her age, that is, of course. But mentally, well, to be frank, Mr and Mrs Taylor, if I may speak in confidence?'

Off they went for a 'speak in confidence'. Mum, Dad and the doctor, huddled in the corner by the cooker, occasionally glancing in my direction, all looking serious and nodding their heads, like people who have to make big decisions, like people who know what's best.

Fragments and snatches of whispers came my way. Things like, '*Can't really be trusted,*' and, '*Such a shame,*' and, '*Barely able to take care of herself, let alone be responsible for a young girl,*' And then, '*Yes, I think so, that would be best,*' and, '*Sad, but inevitable,*' and, '*Meredith can stay here with us. The old lady must have seen it coming – she was talking to us about it, just the other day.*'

It's funny the way they talk about you when they think you're old. They start off quiet, not wanting you to hear, but gradually they get louder and louder, as if they've forgotten you're there and that it's *you* they're talking about. In the end they're all talking about you quite ordinarily, just as if you couldn't understand, as if you were a little baby, who hadn't learned to speak yet and didn't know the language, and all you needed was a pat on the head.

'Right,' Dad said. 'If it's got to be done, then it's got to be done, and the sooner it's done, the better.'

The doctor put his stethoscope away, and then he snapped the lid of the case shut, with a sharp, loud click, almost like a full stop, as if that now put an end to it, and the case had made a decision, too.

'I'd better break the news to Meredith,' Mum said, heading upstairs.

'I'll get the spare bed ready,' Dad said. 'The sheets are in the airing cupboard, are they?'

Mum hesitated. 'It might be better if Meredith spent tonight in Carly's room,' she said. 'She's probably going to be quite upset by this. After all, her granny's her only relative. She might not want to be alone.'

But what about me? I didn't want to be alone either.

'OK,' Dad said. 'I'll put a mattress on the floor next to Carly's bed and bring up a sleeping bag. That'll be all right for a night or so.'

'Right. I'd best go tell her.'

Mum left the kitchen, and then Dad went to get my sleeping bag from the store room and to give it to Meredith. The doctor remained, stiff and embarrassed, and yet trying to be kind.

'It's been a long day . . .' he began. But then he

tailed off. 'I'd better make a few phone calls, Mrs – eh – better call Social Services, get them to ring the home, see if there's a bed there. You'll be fine there – it's a very nice place, very well run, plenty of qualified, caring staff to take care of you.'

If only they would listen, I thought. If only they would listen to me! But nobody does listen. Not to children or to old people. They think that you've imagined everything, that you've made it up.

He went off to make his phone calls from his car.

'Back in a minute,' he said. 'Won't be a tick.'

He could have been a million ticks. I wouldn't have minded. Where were they going to send me? A home? But I belonged here. This was my home. I didn't need another one.

Mum's voice drifted down from upstairs as she broke the 'bad news' to Meredith. Not that it was bad news to her. It was more likely the best news she'd had in fifty years.

'Your granny, Meredith – I know it's upsetting, but frankly, she's rather ill. Her mind. Old people's minds – sometimes they deteriorate. And we all hate to do it, but we feel there's no choice, really. Otherwise, something terrible could happen. A fire, or she might leave the gas on, or the taps running, or she might go wandering off in her dressing gown. She'd be a danger to herself. And to you, too, to be honest. So we'd like you to stay with us for a while. Just till we get things more sorted out, and then a proper decision can be made about your future. Meantime you can sleep in Carly's room. Is that all right, Carly?'

'Oh *yes*, Mum, of *course*, Mum!' my voice

answered, all simpering and creepy and goody two-shoes, and full of being kind to dumb animals and small creatures and those less fortunate than ourselves.

It made me sick just to hear myself.

Mum, Mum! I thought, *Can't you tell? Can't you tell that it's not me! It's someone else. It's my voice, yes, but it's not me in there. Can't you see that?* Then the crying started. It was Meredith. She must have been crying the biggest crocodile tears since crocodiles were invented.

'Oh poor, Granny,' she bawled. 'Poor, poor, Granny. And she was always so kind to me and looked after me so well. Poor, poor, Granny.' And she went on like that for about ten minutes, 'poor-grannying' and sobbing, one after the other, and my mum going, 'There, there, there!'

I wonder I didn't throw up.

The doctor came back, turning his telephone off and putting it away in his pocket. Dad looked into the kitchen. He was carrying a sleeping bag and a pillow.

'Well? Any luck?'

'Yes, fortunately. They can take her in tonight.'

'Where?'

'Merrysides.'

'That sounds all right.'

'It's a good home. Good reputation. They'll be able to look after her. Fully trained staff. It's run by a Mrs Horrington. A very pleasant woman, as I understand.'

More sobbing from upstairs. And then, amidst the tears, I heard Meredith's voice say, 'But we'll be able

184

to *visit* her though, won't we, Mrs Taylor? I'll still be able to visit Granny in the home?'

'Oh, but *of course* you will, Meredith,' Mum reassured her. 'Whenever you want to. We can take you round every day!'

I couldn't believe it! They'd stolen my body. They were putting me in a home. And now they were even proposing to come round and *visit* me. What for? To have a good laugh?

Then I realized. Meredith *had* to say that. It would have seemed wrong if she hadn't. She'd have come across as a callous, unfeeling girl, and they all might have got suspicious.

The tea looked cold as a stone now. I reached out and touched the cup. Dad saw me.

'A fresh cup, Grace?' he asked.

I shook my head.

'Hasn't touched her tea,' Dad said to the doctor.

The doctor picked up his case.

'Must be bad if she hasn't drunk her tea,' he said, in a weak attempt at making a joke and keeping everyone's spirits up. Only he wasn't keeping mine up. My spirits had plummeted.

'I don't like tea,' I said, not angry any more, just icy calm. 'I don't like tea, I don't drink tea, and I am not an old lady. I am not called Grace. I am Carly!'

Dad looked at me sadly. He went to speak to the doctor but— Brrrrrrrg!

The sound of the doorbell prevented him.

'Must be them,' the doctor said.

'Right,' Dad said. 'I expect she'll need some things. Some of her belongings from her house.'

'Yes,' the doctor nodded. 'I expect she will.'

'We can pick her things up later,' Mum said, coming back downstairs. 'I'm sure we can find enough here for an overnight bag.'

The bell rang again, impatient now, in a hurry to get things sorted out.

'Won't be a minute.'

Dad went to get the door. The doctor looked at me. He reached out his hand to help me to my feet.

'Em, I'm afraid, Mrs – eh, it's – it's maybe time – time to – be on our way.'

Our way? *My* way, he meant. People say 'our way' when you're old. But they don't come with you. You have to go 'our way' all on your own.

The stairs creaked as Meredith and the witch who was now me came down to say goodbye. They had to, didn't they? Or that would look funny, too.

I took my walking stick from the umbrella stand. The doctor had taken hold of my arm. I didn't want to go – but what was the use? I was just a little old lady. Other people were there as well, now. A man, and a woman in a kind of nurse's uniform.

'The ambulance is waiting.'

They had come to take me away.

Meredith sprang forwards and put her arms around me.

'Granny, oh, Granny, it's so *sad* to see you go. We've been so happy together. You were so kind to look after me. I'll come and visit you every day.'

I summoned up all my old-lady strength, pushed with all my might and sent her flying across the hall. She banged her head on the wall.

'Ow! Granny! Granny! Why did you do that?'

It was a mistake. I shouldn't have done it. Everyone

was certain I was batty now. Batty and full of temper, an old lady who had to be watched and controlled, or otherwise she might suddenly strike out.

'Come along now, love. This way.'

'I packed you a bag, Grace,' my Mum said. 'Just a few overnight things. We'll bring your own belongings from the house tomorrow. Clothes and books and whatever else you need. You'll feel more at home then, once you have your own momentos and personal things.'

The tears were in my eyes again. I had to go now. Leave my home. Leave my mum and dad and my room and my childhood and my cat and my stick insects and my studies and my computer and all my happy evenings that would never come again.

It was over. My life was over. Stolen, and over. And I would never get it back.

'Come on now, love. No sense in crying. This way.'

No sense in crying? What a strange thing to say. Why would there be *sense* in crying? There wasn't sense in crying; your heart was in crying. What was the sense in music, or pictures, or sunsets, or the way the flowers dance in the wind?

Was sense all that mattered? What was the sense in looking for sense in everything?

They led me towards the door, firm but gentle, the way people are with you when you're old – most of the time, though occasionally, when tempers get frayed, there can be a sudden, vicious and stinging slap.

Only that was to come later.

For now it was all sympathy and understanding and doing what was best.

'Mum!' I turned in the doorway and looked back. 'Can I have Sam?'

She went very pale, and trembled, as if she'd been struck a blow. She looked at Dad and he stared back at her.

'Come on now, love,' the nurse by my side said.

'No, wait a moment. What was that you just said, Grace?'

'Sam. Can I have Sam, please? And I'm not Grace, I'm Carly. And I don't have anything to take with me. Not one single thing that's really mine, to remind me of you and Dad and everything – so can I have Sam?'

There was silence. A long, awful silence, filled with doubt. The two witches looked worried. The nurse, the doctor and the attendant looked perplexed. Mum and Dad looked . . . mystified.

'Sam, Grace? Why would you want Sam? How did you know about Sam?'

Carly, the witch in my body, piped up straight away.

'I must have told her, Mum. I must have mentioned Sam to her sometime.'

I rounded on her.

'Don't you call my mum "Mum"!' I snapped.

The doctor looked at Dad.

'Who's Sam?' he asked.

Dad swallowed, as though his throat were dry, and said, 'He's Carly's teddy bear. She's had him since she was—'

'Since I was two and a half, Dad,' I reminded him.

He nodded, staring at me in wonder.

'Yes, that's right – how – how did you—?'

'I must have mentioned it to her, Dad,' the witch that was me, now said.

'Don't you call my dad "Dad" either!' I told her. Flipping cheek, she had!

The nurse was looking at her watch.

'It is getting late,' she said. 'Time's getting on.'

'Yes,' the doctor said. 'I do have some other visits.'

'I don't have anything,' I said. 'Nothing at all. Please, can I have Sam?'

Mum looked at Dad and then at 'Carly'.

'Carly,' she said, 'I think that maybe when Grace was a girl, she had a cuddly toy too. And it must have had the same name as yours. I think she's back there now, in her mind. Would it be possible, do you think, for you to—?'

The witch – the witch! – actually began to cry.

'Oh, Mum, not *Sam*,' she blubbered. (And she couldn't half put on the waterworks when she wanted to.) 'You can't expect me to give her *Sam*. Anything but *Sam*. Not *Sam*. One of the other cuddly toys, maybe, but not *Sam*, no. He's *special*.'

And behind her, I saw that Meredith was smirking.

'Here you are, Grace,' Dad's voice said. 'Here's Sam for you.'

He was holding up a soft toy. A teddy bear that had been sitting on the hall windowsill. It wasn't Sam at all. Sam was up in my room. It was just some rotten old bear we'd been trying to get rid of for ages.

I snatched it from him and threw it to the ground.

'That's not *Sam*! Sam's up in my room! Under my pillow! That's Sam!'

'We're not going to get anywhere with this,'

189

the doctor said. 'I think we'd better go. She's beyond reason.'

Then it came to me. The one way I could convince them. The one thing I could say to let Mum and Dad know it was really me. It was one thing the witches couldn't know about. Because we never talked about her, not to anyone, ever. Not me or Mum or Dad. She was precious to us. She was ours and ours alone – my baby sister, who had been born too soon and had only lived for a few days.

'Mum,' I said. 'It *is* me. If it isn't me how would I know about Marsha? About how small and perfect and lovely she was, and how her hand was no bigger than my finger, remember? And there wasn't a nappy to fit her she was that little and small. That was right, wasn't it? And she was born with an extra toe, wasn't she? One toe too many. But they said it was nothing to worry about, as they would tie a thread around it, and it would wither away as she grew older. Remember? Only she never did grow older. And we sat and cried in the waiting room. Remember, Mum, remember? We sat and cried in the waiting room, surrounded by all the flowers.'

That did it. I heard her gasp. I saw the doubt and uncertainty cloud her eyes. Words formed, but she couldn't utter them. Then—

'M – Marsha?'

She looked at Dad. She trembled a little and held on to the door to steady herself.

'John, how could she know – about Marsha? It doesn't make sense. It—'

Then I heard a voice. *My* voice.

190

'I told her. I told her about Marsha too.'

We all turned. It was me – Carly.

'Sorry,' she said.

The witch's wits were sharp as knives and quick as fleas. She didn't know who Marsha was, but she knew how to pretend.

'I told her. Sorry, Mum. Sorry, Dad. I didn't mean to. I told her. I was just upset. I just needed to tell someone – old and wise, I thought – and who might understand.'

They believed her. I suppose they had to. It made more sense to believe the lie than to accept the truth. The lie was simple. The truth was hard and complicated.

Mum was looking at me – at Carly rather, the witch in my body.

'You told her – about Marsha – your little sister?'

Her tone wasn't reproachful, just surprised. But what she said and the way she said it told the witch all she needed to know.

'For comfort,' she said. 'That was all, Mum.'

And it was all she needed to say.

Dad put his arm around her and gave her the cuddle and the comfort she needed.

I had played my best and my only card. And somehow I had been outmanoeuvred. I had lost the hand and the game.

It was over.

They helped me outside and into the waiting ambulance. I was so numb and unbelieving that I wouldn't even look at anyone. Not even out of the back window as we drove away.

191

I suppose they waved. I suppose they did. I was too full of anger and unhappiness to care. I began to cry again, sob after sob, as we drove off into the night.

The nurse turned round and patted me on the knee.

'There, there, dearie,' she said. 'There, there.'

My temper flared up again.

'Don't you "There, there" me!' I told her. 'Or I'll knock your block off.'

We drove the rest of the way in silence.

I wished I hadn't said that. Maybe it was my red hair. Some people think that if you've got red hair you've got a short temper. I don't think that's true. Tempers are tempers, they've got nothing to do with hair colour.

And anyway, I didn't have red hair. Not any more. My hair was white.

I'd joined the cauliflowers. In the cauliflower patch. In the Merrysides Home for Retired and Elderly Gentlefolk.

15

Merrysides

So there I was, in the old folk's home. It looked nice enough from the outside, as a lot of places do. There was a board out by the driveway. It read: 'Merrysides Home for Retired and Elderly Gentlefolk. A splendid home in a picturesque environment. Fully trained nurses. Sun lounge. Gardens. Rates negotiable. Holiday Respite Care. Prop. Mrs P. Horrington.'

So yes, it looked all right from the outside, and it sounded all right in theory, and if you'd only been there on a flying visit, you'd have thought it was quite all right, too.

But visitors only got to see the nice rooms. There were other rooms, which weren't so nice, where people tended to get shunted when they were on their own, or when their relatives stopped visiting, or couldn't afford to pay so much any more.

The council paid for me. So I soon ended up in one of the not-very-nice rooms, as the council didn't pay very much.

They came to visit me at first, for a while, like they said they would. But they came to gloat, really, at least Meredith and that girl Carly did.

It wasn't very nice having your own body coming to visit you, standing there waiting till your mum and dad were out of the way chatting to Matron or to Mrs Horrington, (Horrington by name and horrible by nature), and then it would start.

'Oh, look at what a nice room she's got, Meredith!'

'Yes, it *is* nice, isn't it? Nowhere near half as stinky as you'd expect.'

'She's even got her own sink.'

'And her own chair to sit on. And her own window to look out of. So she can watch the world go by.'

Then they would start with their sharp little fingers, going pinch, pinch, pinch. I ended up black and blue after their visits. Sometimes I used to have to take my walking stick to them, to stop the pinching. I was usually too slow to catch them, but I managed to get them once. I bashed Meredith hard on the shins until she yelped. Then I raised the walking stick up and I was just about to whack Carly as well, when I suddenly thought – 'That's *me*! That's *my* body! Those are my shins I'm about to bash!'

And I couldn't do it. Not to my own shins. So I let her get away with it, I suppose.

The visits stopped shortly after that. I heard murmurings outside the room. It was Mrs Horrington talking to my mum and dad.

'A danger to the girls, I'm afraid, Mr and Mrs Taylor,' she said. 'Attacked them with her walking stick. Maybe it might be best to stop the visits for a time, until she's more her old self.'

How could I be my own self when I didn't even have my own body? Anyway, I didn't want to be my *old* self. It was my *young* self I wanted to be.

'Perhaps a course of anti-depressants might be best.'

They tried to give me pills then but, when they weren't looking, I flushed them down the toilet. They never suspect you when you say you want to go to the toilet. They seem to think it's the best place for old ladies. They'd be quite happy for you to spend all day in the lavatory.

It was a shock that first night, though.

I had to have a bath.

You've got to remember that I'd never seen myself without my clothes on. Not the old-lady self I now was.

I cried for ages. I was so wrinkled everywhere. I was like a balloon that had let the air out. Deflated, that was me. I was soggy as a rice pudding in a wet sock.

And when I went to bed that night, I had to take my teeth out and put them in a glass, so that I wouldn't accidentally choke on them, or swallow them while I was asleep.

It was very peculiar having no teeth in. You felt all gummy. I lay in bed for ages, just rubbing my top gums against my bottom ones, and staring at my teeth in the glass. They just sat there and smiled back at me.

I had to soak my teeth every night in this special liquid to keep them clean. Then, in the morning, I'd rinse them off before I put them back in. I had a toothbrush, too, that Mum brought for me. It was a special dentures toothbrush, really hard and rough and down-to-business. It was really odd to be there at the sink brushing your teeth when your teeth weren't actually in your mouth, but you were holding them in your other hand.

One lunchtime they fell out on to my plate, and before I could tell anyone, they'd been taken away and had disappeared into the rubbish chute. It took ages to find them. And I had to brush them for hours to get them clean. Another time there was a mix-up in the bathroom, and somebody else walked off with my teeth and I got theirs. I knew they were the wrong ones as soon as I went to put them in. Trying to have a chew with someone else's teeth is like trying to go for a walk in someone else's shoes. Either they're too small or too big, and neither way is comfortable. And on top of everything else, they tasted of fish. Eeugh!

After that I decided to write my name on my teeth with a biro. On the pink bit that is, not the toothy bit. I wrote, 'These are Carly's teeth. Touch these teeth, and you are dead.'

I suppose I should have written 'Grace' really, because that was what everyone called me now. But I was still Carly to me, and I always would be, till the day I died.

After a while my belongings arrived. Well, *Grace's* belongings, that is. Or what my mum must have thought were her belongings when she cleared out the house where Meredith and her 'granny' used to live.

Three boxes came, and as the porter was busy, Mrs Horrington brought them along to my room herself. She was big enough to carry half a dozen boxes and still balance a chest of drawers on her head and have a carthorse for afters.

'Yours!' she said, dropping the boxes on to the floor and kicking one of them under the bed. There

196

was the sound of a plate or a cup breaking. She didn't seem to hear, or she heard but didn't care.

I looked at the boxes.

'What is it?'

'Your junk,' she said. 'Sent on to you. All the usual rubbish, I suppose. Mouldy old souvenirs and dog-eared photos and that sort of clutter. Just keep it out of my sight, that's all. I don't like clutter, and photos aren't allowed.'

'Photos aren't allowed? *None?*'

'No more than two, anyway. Two photos per mantelpiece per room, and that's all. Otherwise it makes the dusting too hard for the cleaners. They don't like things finicky. So if I see more than two photos up, they go straight in the bin.'

'Don't you think that's a bit harsh?' I said.

She looked at me indignantly.

'Harsh? It's not a *holiday* camp we're running here, you know!' she said. 'It's an old folks' home. You're not here to *enjoy* yourselves. You're here to keep out of the way and stay tidy, and to be as little trouble to anyone as possible. So you just stick to the rules and keep your nose clean and don't go losing your teeth and make sure you don't wet your knickers ever, and we'll get on just fine!'

She headed for the door, and slammed it behind her, leaving me with the boxes.

I peeled one of the lids back and peered inside. There were some old granny clothes in there and some ornaments, and what looked like a pile of dusty, old books at the bottom, brown and uninteresting. I couldn't be bothered to take them out, so I pushed the box into a corner, where it wouldn't be in

197

the way of the cleaners, when they came to do the dusting.

I searched though the old clothes, seeing what there was. They were as dull and frumpy as the ones I had on. And there were some spare pairs of bloomers. I didn't think I'd ever get used to the bloomers. Great big, down-to-your-knees, granny bloomers they were. You could have kept rabbits in them and no one would ever have known.

Shortly after the belongings arrived, the witches came to see me one last time, the two of them, on their own together, one afternoon after school.

'Your granddaughter's here!' a nurse announced, putting her head round the door. 'The dear girl has come to see you, along with her friend. So you haven't been forgotten. Isn't that nice?'

She let them both into the room before I could stop her. I picked up my walking stick and got ready to defend myself.

'Hello, Granny dear,' Meredith said, for the nurse's benefit. Then when the nurse had gone, she got nasty.

'We need to see you, Old Stuff' she said. (And I certainly didn't like being called Old Stuff.) 'Some of our things have gone missing. I think they may have got mixed up with yours.'

At that they grabbed the boxes which had recently arrived, and turned them upside down. Everything fell out, all over the floor. The mess was awful. They kicked and spread everything around, trying to find what they were after. But whatever it was, it wasn't there.

'Must have got put out with the rubbish,' Meredith said, more muttering to herself than talking to anyone. 'Still. It doesn't matter so much if it's been destroyed. Just as long as it doesn't fall into the wrong hands.' She looked at me. I raised up my walking stick – just in case. 'Hands like yours,' she added. 'Wrinkled old goody two-shoe hands.'

Then she turned to her sister, who was sitting there on my bed, in my body, swinging my legs as if she owned the place, and to add insult to injury, she was picking my nose with my finger.

'Don't be so disgusting,' I told her.

'I bet you used to do it!' she sneered.

'I never did!'

'Come on,' Meredith said to her. 'Let's leave the old bat in peace. It must be somewhere else.'

They opened the door and left, trilling, 'Bye, bye, Granny! So lovely to see you! Sorry it's such a short visit!' as they went. But it was all done for the nurse's benefit, just in case she was still within earshot.

'I'm sure they'll be back to see you again soon,' the nurse said cheerfully. 'Isn't it lovely to have young visitors.'

'No,' I thought. But I didn't say so. And anyway, they never came back.

So there I was.

I used to say it to myself all the time.

'So here I am!'

Then I'd look around the room, as if somehow I could find an answer to all my woes, just by looking around the room and saying, 'So here I am.'

Of course there were plenty of other people in the home, but I didn't really make friends with anyone. They were years older than me – inside and out. (Well, inside, anyway.) They had things in common, too. Memories of old places, old songs and tunes, recollections of people who had once been famous, old film stars, days of wars and bombshells falling, of things like that.

I was just a girl inside. I didn't know what they were talking about half the time, nor did I want to either.

So on I drifted, from day to day. Some days I just sat and cried. Other days I just sat. Other days I just cried. And then I didn't cry so much any more. Because what was the use?

Merrysides wasn't all bad – at least as long as Mrs Horrington wasn't around. But when she was there, the atmosphere was terrible. She was just like a bit of grit in your eyeball.

There was a nice lady called Nurse Bartley, who used to organize the sing-songs and hand out soft cakes to eat which you could manage with your gums if you had gone and left your teeth in your room. As I say, I didn't know the words to the songs but I used to hum along.

She also organized dancing, to old-time music. An elderly gentleman with a small moustache asked me to do the waltz with him, and then the tango. But I didn't know how to properly and trod on his feet, and he didn't ask me to dance again after that. I told him I was good at hopscotch, but he wasn't very interested.

Then there was bingo. I tried to get interested in that too, but it just seemed boring, and it wasn't any-where near as good as netball.

Days turned into weeks and then I didn't count them any more, and each day was like the next. First there was breakfast in the morning, followed by TV in the TV lounge. Then there was a cup of tea at eleven. Nobody would believe that I didn't drink tea. They kept giving it to me, regardless. So I started to drink it in the end. I even got to like it. And it helped to wash down the biscuits, which were hard to chew with plastic teeth.

After elevenses, there were activities (nothing too strenuous, mind). There was 'Keep Fit for Old Folks', which you could do sitting down if you wanted to, and there was 'Yoga for the Elderly', only sometimes people fell asleep during that on their exercise mats. One old man came along, convinced that it was 'Yoghurt for the Elderly' and he kept asking where the spoons were, and said he wanted a raspberry one.

If you didn't want to do activities, there was inactivity in the TV lounge, and then it was lunch. After lunch there was TV and snoring, until it was time for afternoon tea. Then there was more TV and more snoring, unless you wanted to do afternoon activities, such as knitting, embroidery and making baskets. Then it was take-your-pills time, for those who were supposed to be taking them. (There was also a take-your-pills time in the morning, and another, just before bed. Some of the residents took so many pills they rattled when they walked.)

After pills there was more TV in the TV lounge followed by dinner followed by TV followed by cocoa. I was always trying to change the channel in the TV lounge, so as to get to see the children's programmes or to watch *Top Of The Pops* or *The Simpsons*. But when I did, everyone moaned, and went, 'What a racket! No, not that again!' And so we had to watch the soaps instead, or even listen to Mrs Horrington playing tunes on her electric keyboard, which was always a painful experience.

Then cocoa was followed by bedtime, followed by tomorrow. Which was usually much the same as yesterday. And tomorrow was followed by another tomorrow, and another one after that.

Now and again there were other things to do. Someone might come round to give a talk, or to show us flower arranging, or to play the accordion and remember the good old days – which, of course, I knew nothing about.

Then suddenly it was Christmas.

Some children came to sing us carols. Mrs Horrington even turned the TV off for that.

'Children have come,' she announced, 'to sing us carols and remind us of the old days when we were young. So pay attention and stay awake, and no snoring.'

The children launched into 'Away in a Manger' then, and several other carols after that. Soon quite a few old ladies were crying, and the old men too. Just quiet crying. Nostalgia, I think it's called.

I couldn't bear to hear the children singing the carols. I went up and hid in my room and held tightly on to my walking stick until they had gone.

Then I had the fall. I don't know what happened, I just tripped on the stairs. I didn't fall far, only a few steps, but there was a searing pain. Nurse Bartley helped me back to my room, but Mrs Horrington was really angry and annoyed, as she had to call the doctor. He said I was lucky I hadn't broken my leg and put me on to these painkillers for a while. He said it was just a sprain, but my ankle was never right after. I couldn't always get about with just the stick any more, and sometimes had to use one of those frames instead. You may have seen them. I'm sure you know the ones. They look like half a bicycle, only without the wheels. Loads of old people have them. Zimmer frames, they're called.

Once I'd had a climbing frame. Now it was a walking one.

One good thing Merrysides did have was a really nice garden, with a huge lawn and flowers, but there was nowhere to sit, not one single bench anywhere.

I asked Mrs Horrington why there weren't any benches.

'Don't want people wandering around outside,' she said. 'You're all far better off in the TV lounge where we can keep an eye on you.'

'But I'd quite like to go out and sit in the garden sometimes,' I said.

She fixed me with one of her looks.

'Well, you *can't*. If you're *that* fond of gardens, you can admire it from your window. And I don't want to hear another word on the subject. Or I'll confiscate your teeth. Not just for a day either. For a whole week. You won't be able to chew anything and you'll have to eat your porridge through a straw. And you'll have a hard job sucking the lumps up. I can tell you that, now!'

And she stomped off down the corridor like a sack with two fat legs.

The only thing I really did have plenty of in that home was lots and lots of thinking time. When the visits and the visitors ceased, when the letters stopped coming, when I was asked (told) not to write any more letters to my mum and dad, pleading with them to take me away from here, saying that I was their daughter, when all that finished and I was utterly old and so completely alone and so lonely I could die, that was the one thing I had.

Thinking time.

And something came to me.

An idea. Or maybe not so much an idea exactly, more a question which needed an answer.

The real Meredith. Where was the *real* Meredith? Trapped in an old lady's body, wasn't she? An old lady's body, just like mine. And stuck in an old people's home somewhere, just like me.

Maybe this one.

16

The Real Meredith

Thinking was all there was to do. For a while I used to write letters, beginning, *Dear Mum and Dad, I know you won't believe this but—*

But I must have written too many of them, because one day the police came round, and Mrs Horrington set a 'private room' aside for a 'little interview'. (I think, at first, she was worried that the police had come for her.)

It was quite a big thing when the police came round to the Merrysides Home for Retired and Elderly Gentlefolk. There hadn't been so much excitement in years, not since the biscuits ran out for afternoon tea and there was nearly a riot. People even stopped watching the big telly in the TV lounge when they saw the squad car coming up the drive.

'The police!' people muttered when they saw the car. 'It must be for Mrs Horrington! They're found out what a nasty piece of work she is, and they've come to take her away at last. And not before time. Maybe they've come to take Cook away too. The way she overcooks the vegetables is practically criminal, anyway.'

But no. They'd come for me. To give me a warning not to write any more letters to Mr and Mrs Taylor (of the mentioned address) addressing them as 'Mum' and 'Dad', as they were finding such things very upsetting, and it was interfering with the proper upbringing of their daughter Carly and her friend Meredith ('Your granddaughter, remember dear?'), who Mr and Mrs Taylor were also looking after *in loco parentis* – whoever that was – and hoping to adopt as their own one day.

I had to stop making the telephone calls as well.

They were very kind really, the two police officers. They were more sad and sorry than angry. They just thought I was a poor old soul whose marbles had all rolled down the manhole.

Mrs Horrington sat in on the interview and looked very strict, as if she'd sprayed herself with extra starch that morning. She assured the police officers that, 'None of this will happen again', and that she would, 'Keep an eye out for her', and 'make sure she doesn't go sneaking out to the postbox at the end of the drive', and that 'she doesn't get her hands on the telephone'.

She was as good as her word, too, and she took all my writing paper and envelopes away, and she pinched what was left of my stamps, too. I dare say she used them on the cards she sent out to people saying, 'Have a rotten Christmas' and, 'Hope your turkey chokes you'.

All she left me to write with were a few pencils and some scraps of paper, which I had rescued when she tore up my writing pad.

It helped to have some writing things, to organize my thoughts. First, I thought about it long and hard, and then this is what I wrote:

1) Once upon a time there were two witches – Grace and Briony.
2) They were sisters, and both growing old.
3) They set out to steal two young girls' bodies, swapping their minds and souls round, so that the two witches could be young again.
4) First they tricked an orphan called Meredith, and the witch Briony stole her body. Then they got rid of her.
5) The witch Briony was now in Meredith's body, and the witch Grace pretended to be her grandmother.
6) In this way they tricked a second girl (me, Carly), and stole her body too and went to live with her parents. When they have been in the stolen bodies for thirteen months, thirteen weeks, and thirteen days, the bodies are theirs for ever, and they get all their powers back and will start in on the witch-craft again.
7) **Fact** – they got rid of the real Carly (me) by getting her put into an old folks' home. They said they got rid of Meredith in the same way.
8) **Question** – assuming they stuck Meredith in a home, which home did they stick her in?
9) **Answer** – I don't know. But it could possibly be this one.
10) **Question** – In that case, is it worth having a look around to see if I can find her?
11) **Answer** – Yes. At least you've got nothing to lose.
12) Next question, and then I'll stop asking them.
13) Good.
14) **Question** – If she (the real Meredith) is in this home, how am I going to recognize her? What's she going to look like?
15) **Answer** – She's going to look like you, stupid. You're both in the witches' old bodies. The witches said they stole sisters' bodies last time. Chances are they would have looked the same. Might even have been twins. So go and see if you can find yourself – an old lady who looks like you!

I sat awhile, peering through my glasses at my piece of paper and wondering about my conclusions.

They seemed to make sense. My spirits rose. But they just as suddenly sank again. If the real Meredith were in this place, surely I'd have seen her by now. In the TV lounge, or the dining room, complaining about the soggy vegetables, or the small helpings, or the dried crusty bits on the knives and forks.

Or maybe not. Some of the residents stayed in their rooms. They were too ill or frail or too fed up to move, and had their meals brought up to them on a tray. So I decided to go exploring, to see who and what I might find.

First of all, I had to give Mrs Horrington the slip. She watched me constantly, ever since the police had been round.

'We don't want you bringing the Merrysides Retirement Home into disrepute,' she said.

I didn't know how she worked that one out. How could anyone bring it into disrepute when it had no repute to start with?

She'd told the other members of staff to keep an eye out for me, too. Even Mrs Horrington couldn't be everywhere at once, though she did have a pretty good try.

I decided that lunchtime would be the best. The home was always busy then with clattering plates and clanking trolleys and big tureens of stewed turnip and pots of mushy peas, and all the other old-fashioned things they used to give us to eat. I don't think they'd ever heard of pizza, and the only time we got chips was when a member of the Royal Family had a birthday.

Anyway, one day, when the gong went for lunch, all the inmates came out of their rooms or the TV lounge or wherever, and traipsed along towards the dining room. They all got a bit more lively when food was in the offing. I joined the throng. Mrs Horrington was behind us, carrying on a bit like a farmer who was taking all the cows in for milking. Some days I used to go 'Moo!' just to get her going. She didn't like it at all.

'Who's that making those mooing noises?' she'd yell. 'This is a well-run, respectable old people's home! It's not a cattle market you know!'

Anyway, there was always a bottleneck as we came to the dining room, and that was where I got my chance. I nipped up the back-stairs and out of sight.

It wasn't nipping like I used to do when I was a girl, it was more old-lady sort of nipping. Very slow nipping. But I was gone before anyone noticed, and I clambered on up the back-stairs, holding on to the handrail for support, as I made my way up to the top floor.

There was a lift, but I didn't want to use it in case I was seen. It took me ages to climb all the way to the top, and I had to stop several times to give my knees a rest and to catch my breath.

At last I was there. I'd decided to start at the top and work my way down. I wouldn't get it all done in one day, but that didn't matter. What I couldn't do today I could do tomorrow. I had nothing else to do, after all. I had all the time in the world.

But then it struck me that no, I didn't. In fact I was now so old and frail that I could probably drop dead at any moment.

I paused to get my breath and to let my heart slow down. It was knocking at my ribs like someone hammering on a nail.

I went to the end of the corridor and tapped on the door of a room. Nothing. No one in there. I went on to the next room and tried again.

'Yes? Who is it?'

But it was the voice of an old man. Not who I was looking for. I moved on. I heard him calling as I went.

'Who's there? Is that my lunch tray? Who's there?'

But I didn't have time to stop and explain.

I tried the next door. Nothing. Empty then. But maybe not. What if somebody was in there, fast asleep? I tried the handle. But the room was locked. On I went. Next room, the next, the next again.

'Yes? Who is it?'

I opened the door. An old lady was in the room. She was sitting up in bed with a bag of sweets. She had her own small television and the remote control was in her hand.

'Meredith?' I said.

'Oh,' she cried. 'A *visitor*! Jennifer, is that *you*, dear? How are you? And the twins? Did you bring them? You've not been for ages.'

'Sorry,' I said. 'Wrong room.'

I made to close the door.

'No don't go. Stay a while,' she cried. 'Stay and talk, whoever you are. It's so long since I've had a visitor. Don't go!'

But I couldn't stay. I would have done, but I simply didn't have the time.

On I went, room after room. Most of them were empty, the others had mostly bedridden old souls in

210

them. They thought I was bringing their lunch trays when they heard my knock, or that I was an unexpected visitor. Some of them were mightily disappointed when it turned out that I wasn't.

I came to the end of the corridor. Well, that was it. If Meredith was here, she wasn't up on this floor.

Down to the next.

As I headed for the stairs, I heard the lift arrive and its doors open. Mrs Horrington appeared, wheeling a trolley with several lunch trays upon it. She entered one of the rooms.

'Lunch!' she said. 'Here you are!'

'What is it today?' the room's occupant asked. It was the old man.

'Mince.'

'I don't like mince. I had mince for breakfast,' he said.

'No, you didn't,' Mrs Horrington told him. 'Your memory's going. You had cornflakes.'

'Well they tasted like mince. Can't I have something else?'

'No. You can't. It's mince or nothing. So eat it while it's hot. It's the best mince that money can buy, this mince. I got half a ton of it at very reasonable price and it has to be eaten. I'll be back for your tray later. And if you don't eat your mince for lunch you won't get any dinner.'

'What's for dinner?'

'Mince.'

Then she was on to the next room. The sounds of her voice and of the rattling trolley grew fainter as I hurried down the flight of stairs to the next level.

I peered round the corner. The coast was clear. I

began from the beginning again, tapping on the doors, trying the door handles, calling Meredith's name.

'Meredith, are you in there? Is that you?'

'*Hello? Hello? Who's that?*'

I'd found her, I'd found her! Had I found her? I opened the door and looked in.

'*Hello?*'

No. I hadn't. The name was right, but nothing else. It must have been a different Meredith. We weren't even the same colour.

'Sorry, sorry to disturb you. Wrong room.'

Same response as before.

'*It's all right. Stay anyway. Stay and visit. Don't run away. It's so long since anyone stopped by for a chat. Don't go, please don't go.*'

But I had to. Time was running out. Lunch would soon be over. Mrs Horrington might notice that I wasn't down there. You wouldn't think she'd notice the absence of one old cauliflower amongst all the other old cauliflowers, but she was cunning and clever and rarely missed a trick.

'Sorry.'

'*No, stay a while, stay.*'

I went on. I did feel sorry for her, but I had to press on. How sad though, I thought, to be old and alone and never to have any visitors apart from Mrs Horrington coming round with plates of mince.

How sad, I thought to be old and all alone. And then I remembered that was just what I was. Unless I could find Meredith.

'Hello?'

Tap, tap. Knock, knock.

212

'Hello?'

The rooms were empty. Two more on this corridor, then it would be down to the next floor, if there was time, or maybe leave it until tomorrow. My hopes were sinking. My legs were sore. My poor old knees were burning.

Tap, tap.

'Hello?'

A reply.

'Hello?'

I turned the handle of the door and peered into the room. There she was. There *I* was. An old lady in a chair. She looked just like me. She could have been my sister.

'Meredith?'

She looked shocked. I saw a name tag on the pocket of her dressing gown. Mrs Horrington sometimes stuck them on people so she could remember their names. (Sometimes so that *they* could remember their names.) The name tag said 'Briony'. But that was only the name of her outside.

'Meredith?'

The old lady stared at me. She didn't move from the chair, but she seemed to recoil in fear.

'You! *You!*'

She went to reach for the alarm bell cord. (Every room had an alarm bell, though the staff were never that quick to answer them. They might not turn up for days.)

'Help!' she cried. 'Nurse, nurse! Come quick. It's the witches again! Who stole me! It's the witch!'

I stopped her just in time, by moving the cord out of her reach.

'Meredith?' I said. 'Is it *you* in there? Is it the *real* you?'

She looked at me, still wondering and afraid.

'Who *are* you?' she said. 'You're one of the witches!'

'No, I'm not,' I said. 'I'm a girl. Just like you are. I've been stolen too. They've taken my body just like they took yours. My name's Carly.'

'Carly?'

'Yes. Carly. Short for Scarlet. I used to be young, and go to school, and I had red hair and freckles and a mum and dad and a stick insect and podgy bits, but I'm sure they'd have gone away in the end. And I know all about you, how you were an orphan and the witches tricked you – at least if that part of the story they told me is true.'

'Yes, it is,' she said. 'But how do you know? No one ever listens – no one ever believes. They just think I'm a poor old woman who's lost her mind.'

'Me too,' I said. 'Me too.'

And I started to cry – in sorrow for what had happened to me, and in happiness at having found someone in the same boat, someone who would believe and understand. I reached out to touch Meredith, just to make sure she was real. She reached out, too, and took my hand.

'Carly,' she said. 'Carly? Red hair and freckles?'

'Yes,' I said. 'And I've seen you – the *real* you. You as you should be. You're tall and willowy with dark brown hair, and you're able to do cartwheels and handstands, and you're as fast as a rabbit and as free as a bird.'

'Yes!' she cried. 'That's me, that's *me*! Where am I? Where did you see me? What am I doing now?'

214

'Well, believe it or not,' I said, 'you're living at my house. You're my best friend.'

And that was exactly what she became.

Up until then, Meredith had hardly left her room. But after that, we became inseparable. I don't think Mrs Horrington liked it. She didn't like old people talking together and having friends. It was too disorderly.

'Be quiet and watch the TV, will you!' she'd snap. 'This TV cost a lot of money. It's very big and it's very good, so you'd better watch it. And if you all behave yourselves properly, I might even turn it on.'

We just ignored her. If we couldn't talk in the TV room, we would go and talk somewhere else. If the weather was fine we might go out into the garden. There were still no benches, but we would lean on our walking sticks or rest on our Zimmer frames, and talk until we got too tired, or it grew too cold, or the rain would drive us inside.

We even tried to do young things together, like girls our age ought to have done. We organized a skipping rope, made out of garden twine, but we were both so old and frail that by the time we had managed to swing the rope above our heads we were too tired to jump over it.

We had some good games of I-Spy though, and some quiet rounds of hopscotch out in the garden – but nothing too taxing. And then for a few days there was mad talk of us saving up our pensions and getting a pair of rollerblades, or a skateboard. But we realized that at our age, and in our condition, rollerblades would probably have been suicide, so we just asked Nurse Bartley to buy us some chocolate instead. Which she very kindly did, along with a copy of the *Beano*. She didn't ask why we wanted it. I expect she just though we were getting old.

And we would visit each other, too. Meredith would come to my room, or I would go to hers. We'd spend hours and hours, just sitting there talking about the old days, when we were girls.

Just like real old ladies do.

Sometimes, as we talked, one of us might find that there was a catch in her voice, or that the tears were on their way. But the other one would realize and say, 'Now, now. It's not so bad. At least there's the two of us now. At least we've got each other.'

My worst nightmare was that Meredith would die before me, and leave me alone again, and I wouldn't be able to talk to her any more. But then if I died first, she would be left alone, and that wasn't very nice either.

'Maybe we'll go together,' she said.

'Yes,' I said, 'I hope so.'

But then, other times, we'd get angry. So, so angry. Livid. Fuming. Furious.

'When I think of those two witches—'

'When I think what they've *done*!'

'When I think of what they've *stolen*!'

'When I think of them in my house, in my room, with my poor mum and dad!'

'And what have they got in store for *them*?'

'Exactly!'

'It makes my blood boil.'

'Mine, too.'

'Only I can't let it boil too much, or I'll have a heart attack and die.'

'That's the problem.'

'So we'd better calm down then.'

'You're right.'

At other times, we would think the unthinkable, and dream of the impossible.

'Say we could steal our bodies back.'

'If only we could get *out* of here.'

'If only we knew some witchcraft ourselves.'

'If only there was a spell!'

'If only!'

But there was no spell that we knew of. And so the time went by, and Meredith and I, who were already so old, grew even older and slower, and more frail and infirm. And the slow, slow days turned to slow, slow weeks and then months had gone by since my arrival.

'I'll be twelve this year,' I said.

'Me too,' said Meredith. 'And the year after that, thirteen. Just imagine – a teenager.'

My eyes seemed to be growing dimmer. I was sure I needed new glasses. But Mrs Horrington said they were just dirty, and I probably only needed to clean them, or I should go and get a magnifying glass. So I never got any new glasses, and just had to make do.

One day I had the idea that maybe Meredith and I could share a room together, and then neither of us would be so lonely. I suggested this to Mrs Horrington, expecting her to say no, but her eyes lit up with greed at the suggestion.

'Certainly,' she said. 'Why not! I could get another old person in then, and make even more money – that is – if it makes you happy, dear. The welfare of my residents is my only concern. Yes, you share with your friend.'

She looked around the room.

'Yes, it's easily big enough for two beds in here,' she said, 'if you budge up a bit. In fact there's probably room for half a dozen at a pinch. You haven't got any other friends you'd like to move in with you?'

'No,' I said firmly, 'just the one.'

'All right,' she said, disappointed. 'I'll get the porter to put a second bed in. You'll just have to move your junk.'

I wondered what she meant. I didn't have any junk to move. Apart from – Oh yes, the boxes. The ones that contained Grace's possessions. They were still there in the corner, all covered in dust.

The porter moved them out of the way, to make room for the bed for Meredith. Then he moved the bed itself, and under it he found a third box. It must have been pushed under there, ages ago, and I had forgotten all about it.

'Where do you want this box?' the porter said.

'With the others, I suppose,' I said. 'Just put it out of the way.'

He went to pick the box up, but it was only cardboard and the bottom gave way. Books and ornaments and souvenirs spilled out all over the floor.

'Whoops,' he said. 'Sorry about that. Here you are, I'll get them.'

He went to gather everything up, but suddenly a bell rang for him and he had to go. It was probably some minor emergency. Somebody stuck in the bath again, or fallen out of bed.

He left us to ourselves.

'Well,' Meredith said. 'We'd better do it.'

So down we got on to our rickety, old knees, our backs creaking and our leg joints crackling like sparklers.

We began to sort the mess out and to straighten everything up.

'Look at this stuff,' I said. 'This must have belonged to the witches.'

It was nothing useful though. Just junk, old magazines, books – not very interesting ones either.

But then Meredith pulled a book out from where it had slid under the chest of drawers. It was a large, brown, heavy book, with a metal clasp on it, and on the binding was its title, in faded gold leaf.

The title was 'Necromancy'.

Meredith looked at it.

'*Necromancy*? What does that mean?'

But I could hardly answer her. My heart was beating fast. I really thought it was the end that time, I honestly did. I took long, deep breaths to calm myself.

'Meredith,' I said. 'This book belongs to the witches.'

'So what's in it?' she said. 'What's inside?'

'*Spells*,' I said. 'It's a book of spells.'

She looked at me. I looked at her.

'Do you think—?' she began.

'Let's see,' I said.

I flipped back the heavy metal clasp, and the book fell wide open. And as it did, something fell from it, a few closely written pages, in a thin and spidery hand.

'It's Grace's handwriting,' Meredith said. 'I recognize it.'

They were pages from a diary.

The diary of a witch.

So there it was. Even a witch has a mind and a heart and a desire to express her thoughts to someone – if only to the pages of a journal.

It was just a fragment we found, a few torn pieces. The edges of the paper were blackened with flame, as if she had burnt the rest. Maybe she had, knowing that a new life was on its way; she had burnt it like a bridge behind her; a bridge which could now never be re-crossed. There could be no going back. Or could there?

I looked at the date. It was dated just over six months ago. Back when I was still me.

I'm getting old now, it read. *My powers are waning, waning like the moon. I don't have much time. I can no longer enact the more powerful spells. I need to accomplish everything now by subterfuge and trickery. I can only do the fast-asleep and the drugged spells. I am no match, otherwise, for a young and active mind. I need to be young – young. I need a young body, and soon. If I leave it much longer it will be too late. I won't be able to accomplish the transformation at all. All my powers will have gone. I need to find someone young and vulnerable, isolated and lonely, perhaps. Someone trusting and eager to believe. Yes. Lies, pretence and deception – they are my best friends, now.*

We each need a new body, my sister and myself. And she already has hers. But not me. It was so much easier in the old days, when children left school at the age of twelve, or never went at all. It was easy pickings then, before all these rules and regulations. Children were easy to come by then, all alone, roaming the streets, they were there for the taking.

Bah! What does it matter? Just as long as we find someone. We need a body each, yes. And a good home, too. Plenty to eat and someone to look after us. At least until we get our powers back.

Thirteen months.

That's the danger.

Having to be in the new body a full thirteen months, thirteen weeks, and thirteen days.

Always the danger that they'll find the spell in the meantime. The spell to cast you out again. But no, it's well-hidden. They'll never find that. Ignorance is bliss - for us anyway, if not for them. What they don't know can't hurt them - and more importantly, it can't hurt me. And even if they found the spell, so what? What are the chances of the conditions ever being right? Not one in a million. Not a snowball's chance in a furnace.

But when that thirteen months, weeks and days are over.

Ha, ha! Hee, hee! Tiddly poo, tiddly pee.

What fun then! When you take full possession. When you can never be evicted. When the body is for ever yours.

Magic and witchcraft, then all right.

Oh, what a wonderful feeling that is - of all the powers returning. How they fill you with warmth from the inside out. Hot chocolate on a cold winter's day. Oh, what a feeling when the powers come back, and you can do the magic again. The real magic. The real deep, dark, wicked magic. Thick as toffee, swirling like snow. Oh, what we sisters won't do, then.

221

Start with them.

Yes. The girl's parents. That Carly girl's parents. Start with them. Just to get our hand in. Just to warm up a little. What will we do to them when the powers come back?

Umm. I know.

First we'll make their fingers disappear. One by one. Fingers, to keep my hand in, that'll be nice. Start with the little fingers, then all the way to the thumbs. Till all that's left is stumps.

Won't they be surprised? Won't they just be so surprised? Then the toes next. One by one. Big piggies first, then the little ones. All gone to market until there's no more piggies at all.

Then what? No fingers, no piggies . . . umm . . . no lips, maybe? Make their lips go away, or seal them up tight with magic so the neighbours won't hear the cries. Then what? Any ideas, sister? Any ideas? Come, think your thoughts to me, give me your mind. What's that? What's that you say? Yes, yes. I think so. Yes, yes. Hair on fire. Yes, all smouldering away. Then what? Then what shall we do? The spell to close their eyes up tight? Yes, yes. I like that. Mouths that can't speak and eyes that can't see and maybe ears that cannot hear, either. Yes. And no little piggies and no little fingers, and all their hair just little bits of ash, and nothing but stumps in their shoes.

And then what shall we do to them, sister? Then what shall we do? Do tell, do tell—

There was no more. But that was enough. It was enough to fill me with a greater fear and dread than any I had known. Mum and Dad – and what the witches had planned for them. Thirteen months.

Thirteen weeks. And thirteen days. That was all it took. Once they had your body that long, you could never get them out, and they had their full powers back. And the witch in Meredith's body – well, she must have been in there quite some time, already. Her full powers would soon be returning. Possibly any week, any day now.

And when they did.

So it wasn't just me any more. It wasn't just me and it wasn't just Meredith. Mum and Dad were in danger, too. Mum and Dad most of all.

17

Cloudless and Cleare

We turned the pages of the book and began to read.

Spells, spells, there were all kinds of spells. How to make yourself invisible with a silken handkerchief; how to confound all your enemies with a little wax doll and a couple of pins; how to make people fall in love with you and worship the very ground you walked on, so that you could spurn them and break their hearts, and be revenged on them for treating you badly.

Spells, spells, all sorts of spells, for big things and little. Impossible sounding spells, a lot of them – spells for flying through the air, spells to make your hair grow when your head had gone bald, spells to make your warts vanish, spells to make them appear on somebody else – right on the tips of their noses.

Most of them were wicked, evil spells. It was a witch's book of magic, all right. They were spells of misery and spells of revenge; spells to steal and to spirit away; spells to turn beautiful people ugly and make sweet things sour. Spells to turn wine into vinegar; spells to kill the crops and to bring bad harvests; spells to curse your enemies; spells to bring disaster; spells to wither people's limbs and to give them nothing but sorrow.

Spells to steal their bodies and their souls.

'*There*!' Meredith said.

'Where?'

'*There*! I've found it.'

'Let me see.'

We had forgotten how old we were. We were lying on the floor with the book open, and our legs in the air behind us, just like in old pictures of children reading books by cosy fires.

Meredith pointed with her finger and I read the words to myself. I knew them. I'd seen them before.

'That's the spell they used on *me*,' I said. 'But it's no good for us. We can't use that one back on them.'

'Why not?'

'The person whose body you want to steal – or steal back in our case – has to be drugged and fast asleep and in the same room. No chance of that.'

'No,' Meredith agreed. 'Turn the page. Maybe there's something else.'

We leafed through the book. Its pages were ragged, as though they had once been cut roughly with a paper knife. The paper was stiff and dry too, with brown spots and patches, mottled with time, just like my hands and skin.

'Look in the index.'

There wasn't one. And the spells didn't really seem to be in any kind of order either. We went on turning the pages, staring at the spells though our thick spectacles, sucking on our false teeth, just like they were long-lasting gobstoppers.

'Here!' Meredith said. 'Here's one. Look at this.'

I looked at where she was pointing. The heading at the top of the page read, *Bodie and Soul, for the Wide*

Awake and Conscious Exchange of, and for when Souls are Unwilling.

It seemed daft to me. When would Souls ever be Willing – certainly not when they were going to get the worst of the bargain.

I read on.

'*First,*' the spell read, '*picke your nighte.*'

Meredith and I stared at each other.

'What does that mean?' she asked. '*Picke your nighte*? Is that like picke your nose or something?'

'Maybe it's all explained as you go along,' I suggested. So we read further.

'*First picke your nighte, and make that a leape nighte with a full moone in the skye—*"

'What's a *leape nighte*?' Meredith said. 'And why have all these words got an extra 'e' on the end?'

'It's how people wrote in those days, I suppose,' I said. 'And a *leape nighte* must be the extra night – you know – in a leap year. February the 29th.'

We stared at each other again.

'Run and fetch a calendar,' Meredith said.

Run?

I could hardly stand up. We'd been lying on the floor for so long, turning the pages of the book, that I'd gone as stiff as a plank.

'Help!' I said. 'I've gone geriatric.'

We managed to get up eventually, and took the calendar down from the wall. We sat on the bed to consult it.

'Well?' Meredith asked. 'Is it or isn't it? Because leap years only come round once every four years. And if it isn't a leap year this year, and we've got to wait another one or two or even three before we get another chance to use the spell – well, we've had it. I don't think I'm going to live another three years, not in this old carcass. I feel as if I might peg out tomorrow.'

It was nearly the end of January, then. I turned the leaf of the calendar with hope and fear in my heart.

Yes! It *was*! A leap year! There it was, tagged on to the end of the month – the extra date of February the 29th!

We looked at each other, wanting to celebrate, but afraid to get too happy too soon.

'What else does the spell say?'

'I'll get the book.'

We put the book down on the bed and carried on reading the spell.

'—*Make that nighte a <u>true</u> full moone nighte, and make it cloudless and cleare*—'

'What's the calendar say?'

'*Yes!* Full moon! Right on the 29th! Yes!'

'What about the *cloudless and cleare* part?'

'We can't do anything about that. We just have to take a chance and hope for the best. Read the rest.'

'OK.'

She read on.

'—*Then make the time a midnighte time, between the first bell and the last*—'

'What's that mean?'

'Means you have to start the spell on the first stoke of twelve midnight, and finish saying it before the twelfth stroke rings, I suppose. What's the rest?'

'Not much more. I'll read it out.'

She turned to the book again.

'*—Encircle those you would ensnare in a golden band, continuous and unbroken. And then saye these wordes—*'

And then there was the spell itself – surprisingly short – a rhyme only a few lines long.

Meredith sat looking thoughtful, clicking her false teeth. It was a habit she had got into. She would shift them with her tongue so that they clacked together. It could be quite irritating if she did it for long.

'A golden band,' she said. 'Continuous and unbroken. Where would we get that from?' She read the line again.

'*Encircle those you would ensnare in a golden band, continuous and unbroken—*' This is two witches we're talking about, Carly. How can we encircle them in a band of gold? All I have is a small neck chain. What sort of gold band does it mean?'

I had an idea.

'Do you think—?'

'What?'

I stood up and tottered over to the wardrobe.

'What are you doing?'

I opened the door and there it was. My box of knitting, it contained a half finished scarf and some balls of wool and several knitting needles.

'Knitting?'

I'd decided to take it up to pass the time, but after half a scarf I abandoned the idea as it was making my arthritic fingers ache too much. Nurse Bartley had brought the wool for me.

And there it was, several balls of it in different colours – green, mauve, speckled grey, silver, light blue – and *gold*.

'*Gold!*'

'*Gold!*'

But then Meredith looked doubtful and dismayed.

'It's not *real* gold though, is it? Just gold coloured.'

'Maybe that's all it has to be,' I said. 'Look, the spell doesn't say a band of *gold*, it says a *golden band*. It's the *colour* that's important, isn't it? It doesn't have to be actual gold, just the right colour.'

Meredith seemed dubious, but had to concede that I might be right.

'Hmm, maybe,' she said. 'Maybe.'

'There's nothing to lose by trying, is there? If the spell doesn't work, and we're still stuck in these old ladies' bodies and in big fluffy slippers with pom-poms on top, we're no worse off. At least we'll have tried.'

'OK. We've got about—' she looked at the calendar '—four weeks.'

And then a thought seemed to come into Meredith's mind. She took down the calendar and she grabbed a pencil and a piece of paper, and she began to do some sums. She checked the sums once, then she checked them again. And then she checked them a third time, so that there could be no mistake.

'What is it?' I said. 'What's wrong?'

She had turned ghastly pale by now and she clutched at my arm.

'Carly! I forgot! It's not just *us*! The spell! It *has* to work. It *has* to be done or—'

'Or *what?*'

'The time will be up! The witch will have been in my body for thirteen months, weeks and days on March 1st!'

229

'What!'

'Yes! The day after the leap year day. The witch in my body will have been there the full time. She can do whatever she likes – to your mum and dad. Remember, the fingers and the stumps? And as for me, I'll never get back in again. Never, never, never! I'll be old until I die. And you'll be next.'

My *mum and dad*! They would be at the witch's mercy. She could turn them into toads, slaves, dung beetles, zombies, all but suck their brains out and control them like puppets on strings. And Meredith, poor Meredith – there would be no hope left at all.

'Then it has to be done.'

'It has to be.'

'February the 29th.'

'What day is it?'

'A Saturday.'

'Four weeks this coming Saturday it is, then.'

'One thing?'

'What?'

'How do we get *out* of here? How do we get round to my house to encircle it in the band of gold and to rescue our bodies from the witches? How do we get away from Mrs Horrington?'

Meredith clicked her dentures.

'There's only one thing for it, Carly,' she said. 'We'll have to go over the wall.'

18

Over the Wall

It was easier said than done, but we had four weeks to plan it. Mrs Horrington was always on the look-out for old ladies wandering aimlessly about the corridors of the home. She had even begun to issue people with identity badges, with their name and room number upon them.

'Think of them as a fashion accessory,' she said. 'Just look upon that safety pin as a nice piece of jewellery. There's no need to forget your name and room number now, as it'll be there on your chest, and we'll all know where you belong. We don't want anyone going wandering out, do we, and ending up under a bus. We have an enviable record here at the Merrysides Retirement Home and we'd hate for any-one to go missing. Your relatives would be so upset. And obviously, if you disappeared, they wouldn't want to pay the fees any more, which would be sad for us all. So let's keep an eye on you, shall we?'

For additional security, Mrs Horrington also had Rotwee to help her. Rotwee was a big, nasty looking Rottweiler, and when it grew dark she would let him loose out in the garden.

'To deter burglars and to stop anyone from breaking in,' she said.

But we were more worried that he might stop us from breaking out.

'The dog's going to be a problem,' Meredith said, as we drew up plans for our escape. 'What are we going to do about him? I don't fancy climbing over the wall with him snapping at my bloomers. Not at my age. I'm eighty-five if I'm a day. And there's no way we can outrun him, is there? Not on Zimmer frames.'

'Perhaps I could belt him with my walking stick,' I said.

'Just make him angrier. Or he might start barking and Mrs Horrington would hear him and come out to see what was up.'

'Then we have to keep him quiet somehow,' I said.

'How?'

'Food. Hang on, what day is the 29th, again?'

'A Saturday.'

'Then it'll be sausages for tea. Fish on Friday remember, sausages on Saturday, and mince and cabbage the rest of the time.'

'The dog will probably like sausages.'

'But so do I. They're the only things I *do* like.'

'Can't be helped. We've got to keep the dog quiet.'

'OK. But how do we get out of the room?'

'Like this. We wait until it's lights out, then we get dressed in our warmest clothes. We put on all our old-lady things, our woolly hats and our thickest support tights and our warmest bloomers and our most sensible shoes. Not forgetting our gloves and scarves, as we have to look after ourselves at our age, and we can't take any chances.'

232

'And then?'

'Then we strip the beds and we knot the sheets together and we tie them to something heavy – like to the radiator or a bed, maybe. Then we shin out of the window, throw the dog the sausages to keep him quiet, nip over the wall, and we're away.'

I suppose for the moment I'd simply forgotten how old I was, and how inappropriate was my choice of words.

Shin. Nip. Run!

It isn't that easy to shin and nip and run, not when you're way past eighty.

But we could try. We could try.

It was bitterly cold, that February evening of Saturday the 29th. The cold was doubly cold, as there were few clouds in the sky to keep the heat in. But that was just as we wanted it. We wanted a clear sky and a visible full moon, and there it was, lighting up the gardens of the Merrysides Home for Retired and Elderly Gentlefolk. From our window we could see Rotwee, Mrs Horrington's Rottweiler, pacing the grounds in an effort to stay warm.

You wouldn't even have left a dog out on a night like that.

Not unless you were Mrs Horrington, of course.

We were dressed up in our old-lady survival gear, clad in several thick layers, wearing half a dozen jumpers and extra socks. We had even put newspapers up our vests to keep out the frost.

'Got the sausages?' Meredith said.

I patted my pocket. There were six cold sausages there wrapped in a greasy napkin. We had eaten

233

one sausage each to keep our strength up, and had smuggled the others out for the Rottweiler.

Meredith was knotting sheets together.

'Plenty of knots,' I said. 'We'll need something to hold on to on the way down. Make a kind of ladder out of it. The knots can be the rungs.'

I was worried about climbing out of the window. It wasn't far down to the ground. Only about ten feet or so. But it might as well have been a parachute jump away. I was afraid I'd fall and crack something. My old bones had seemed to be getting thinner recently. It was as if I'd been crumbling away.

'That happens to people as they get old,' Meredith had told me. 'You need extra calcium. Ask for more milk.'

But Mrs Horrington didn't believe in more. She thought it was bad for the character and led to self-indulgence.

Meredith tied the end of the sheet around the leg of the bed.

'Will it hold?' I asked, worried it wouldn't

'I should think so,' she said. 'Let's face it, we don't weigh much.'

And that was true. We weren't like the big, fat old ladies you sometimes get, we were the small crumbly ones, who peck at their food, and look like birds.

'Who'll go first? Me?'

'If you like. But what about the Zimmer frames. Won't we need them?'

'All right.'

We threw the Zimmer frames out of the window, aiming them at the bushes so that when they landed they wouldn't clatter.

234

Then it was my turn. I sat nervously on the windowsill, took hold of the knotted sheets, and gingerly lowered myself over.

'Are you all right?' Meredith whispered above me.

'I think so. But I shouldn't really be doing this, not at my—' I lost my grip and slid down the sheets to land with a bump on the ground below '—age!'

'You all right?'

'I think so.'

'Nothing cracked?'

I checked. 'No. I'm all right. Just winded.'

'OK. Here I come too.'

'Wait, wait, wait!'

'What?'

'The book, with the spell in it!'

'Oh my – if we'd forgotten that.'

'You're getting so absent-minded, Meredith!'

'I know. It's my age.'

She leaned out of the window to pass me the book, but I couldn't reach it, so she let it fall. I caught it, but the thing nearly knocked me over. I swayed but kept my balance, and when I looked up again, Meredith was climbing down the knotted sheets. I could see right up her dress. She was wearing the most enormous knickers.

'Come on,' I hissed. 'Before someone sees us.'

But someone already had seen us – Rotwee the Rottweiler. He was bounding and rampaging over the lawn like a lion after a gazelle. Only he was more the kind of lion which specialized in eating old ladies.

'Give him the sausages!'

I fumbled in my pocket. Where were they? They weren't there.

'Carly, quick! Quick!'

Now where were they? Where had I put those sausages? I couldn't remember a thing these days. I knew what I was doing one minute, and then the next . . . Once I'd had an old head on young shoulders, now it was a young mind in old brains, and those brains were becoming forgetful.

Where for the life of me had I put those sausages? I hadn't eaten them, had I? No – of course not. I was looking in the wrong pocket.

'Carly! Hurry up!'

I pulled the sausages out and threw them to the ground. Just in time. The Rottweiler screeched to a halt, throwing up dust. He leapt on the sausages and started ripping them to bits.

'That'll keep him busy for a bit. Now let's go!'

I set off. But Meredith called me back.

'Walking frame, Carly! Don't forget!'

Oh yes! We needed that.

I got my Zimmer frame from the bush and Meredith got hers. I tucked the book of spells under my arm and we set off across the moonlit lawn. The sky was clear and almost cloudless. We could easily see where we were going, even with our old eyes. The bad part was that Mrs Horrington would see us if she happened to look out of the window.

The dog ignored us, and carried on chewing at his sausages. He obviously thought we were friends of his now, but quite how long this friendship might last I didn't care to think. I suspected it would only last as long as the sausages did.

We were nearing the gates now and the railings of the fence. They were set into the stonework of a low wall, and reached up to a height of about two or three metres. A padlock held the gates shut tight.

'Give me your Zimmer frame,' Meredith said.

I handed it over, keeping a tight hold of the book. I glanced back at the dog. He was growling now. Half his sausages had gone.

'Come on. Before he finishes them. Hurry up, Meredith. If he starts to bark, we've had it.'

Meredith laboriously wedged one of the Zimmer frames on top of the other to form a kind of ladder by the railings.

'The book! How'll we get it over?'

'Don't need to,' I said. 'I can push it through.'

And I did. I pushed it through, between two railings, and it fell on to the pavement with a gentle thud. For a second the dog looked up from his sausages, his ears pricked up, and then he went back to chomping.

'You go first, I'll steady the frame.'

I took a step towards it and then stopped, suddenly.

My heart sank. Right to the depths of my boots. Right down to the very depths of the deepest boots imaginable, the deepest diver's boots at the bottom of the deepest ocean.

The *wool*! We'd forgotten the *wool*! The golden wool! The spell wouldn't work without it. No wool, no witches, no salvation. And how could we go back for it now? With only two sausages left and the dog at our heels? How could we get back into our room?

It was too far up, too high. I'd never be able to clamber back up those knotted sheets, not with my arthritis, not at my age.

'Meredith—'

'Yes?'

'Meredith – the wool – I haven't got the wool.'

A bright smile crossed her wrinkled old face. Her false teeth looked pearly white in the moonlight.

'It's all right,' she said. 'I have. It's in here.' And she patted the pocket of her lumpy old coat. 'Now let's get going before we freeze to death. It's so cold out here, and at our age the frost gets right into your bones.'

I started to climb. It was hard work, but at least it warmed you up. My old bones creaked like timbers, but I got there in the end.

I sat on the top of the railings, feeling very unsafe. I knew that it wasn't really, but it seemed like a long way down.

'Your turn!' I said to Meredith. 'Come up now.'

Meredith started to climb. She began well, but soon tired and had to pause for breath.

'Don't wait too long, Meredith,' I reminded her. 'We've got to be there before midnight. Or it'll be too late.'

She nodded and started to climb again. Soon she was up on the top of the railings with me.

'Now the hard part,' I said. 'Getting down!' It was a long way down to the pavement on the other side. We couldn't possibly risk jumping it, we'd have broken into a hundred pieces, like china plates. 'OK. Here goes, then. Wish me luck.'

I clambered over to the other side of the railings,

238

then holding on tightly to one of them, I slid down it, like a fireman on a pole suddenly called out to an emergency. The low wall stopped me. From there it was just a small step down to the pavement.

'You OK?'

'Yes. Made it. You'll be all right if you take it slowly.'

The dog was starting to growl again. I could see him in the moonlight, nosing around for morsels.

Meredith began her descent.

'Come on!' I urged her. 'Come on! Come on!'

And then she was beside me, both feet firmly on the ground.

I picked up the book.

'Ready, then?'

'Ready.'

'Come on, then. This way.'

We bustled on along the road, as fast as our old legs would take us.

'I wish I still had my walking frame.'

'Me too.'

'Or something to eat.'

'Yes.'

'Like a sausage.'

'All gone, I'm afraid.'

'Well, never mind.'

'Won't be long now.'

'What's the time?'

'Five past eleven.'

'Let's go, then. Quick! Let's go. There's no time to waste.'

We turned the corner at the end of the road. I looked back once towards the Merrysides Home for

Retired and Elderly Gentlefolk. Most of the lights were off, but one light was still burning – in Mrs Horrington's office. I heard a dog bark once or twice. Maybe it wanted sausages.

19

Onwards

It was cold. Teeth-chatteringly cold. And they chattered worse than anything when they were false ones. We bustled on, as old ladies do.

'Which way, now?' Meredith asked.

'Down here. We'll take a short cut through the centre and then follow the path through the park.'

I'd never been out so late before. Not without my mum and dad, and not in town, not on a Saturday night.

It was amazing. The centre of town was alive with lights and cars and commotion. And all the people were young. Young and boisterous, rowdy and in high spirits, all in search of a good time. They spilled out of the doors of pubs and clubs, and moved on to others. Cars tooted, people laughed. There was the smell of beer and chips and hamburgers in the air. A crowd came out of the cinema. There was a big queue for a night-club, snaking out along the pavement. There were men in white shirts and dark suits standing by the doorways to see that there wasn't any trouble.

It was all so bewildering and frightening – for an old lady.

'Careful!'

'Excuse us!'

'Pardon me!'

There was a crowd around a hamburger van, and further down the road another crowd by a kebab shop. The smell of food made me hungry, but I had no money, and anyway, there wasn't the time.

Some of the young people stopped and stared at us. I suppose we must have been quite an unusual sight in that part of town, at that time of night.

'Hey look! Two old ladies! Are you out clubbing, love? Going to a rave, are you? Off dancing?'

'Bit early for church, ladies!' someone else called out. 'Doesn't start till tomorrow morning. Getting there early, are you, to be sure of a good seat?'

They didn't mean any harm, I suppose, but it was scary just the same.

'Ignore them,' I said to Meredith. And we bustled on.

'Let's have a look at your book, love!' a voice called. A hand seemed to appear from nowhere and went to take the spells book. I held on to it tightly and moved it out of reach.

'Aw!' The voice was full of mock disappointment. 'I only wanted a look.'

Then we were away. The lights of the town centre were behind us, and we were soon in the dark silence of the park.

Our sensible shoes clattered on the pathway. But there were other noises too, rustling noises, tip-toeing, someone-following noises, only when you turned there was nobody there. It was only your imagination. I felt scared and knew Meredith did too. It was being so old that did it. You felt that if

242

anything happened, you wouldn't even be able to run away.

'What's the time?'

'Half past eleven?'

'How far now?'

'Nearly there.'

Frost was settling over the grass and the trees and the roof of the park shelter. That was something else to be afraid of too – ice and slippery pavements, falling and breaking your hip and never being able to—

'This way, Meredith – shortcut – down here.'

It all came back to me, as if I'd never been away. There was the lane. There was the post box on the corner. There was my street. There was my house. There was my—

It wasn't *there*!

No, not the house. The house was there. It was the *car*. Mum and Dad's car. It was nowhere to be seen. They weren't in! Not at home. We'd never thought of it. Not once in all our planning. How could we not have foreseen it and considered it as a possibility? That we would go to the house to make the spell— but the witches wouldn't even *be* there.

I stopped. I must have looked deadly pale. Meredith was staring at me.

'What's the matter? What's *wrong*?'

'There's no one there. The car's gone. The house is in darkness. There's no one in!'

Salvation! It turned the corner. There it was! They hadn't changed it. Same old car, just a few more dents in it. Same old Mum and Dad – maybe a few more dents in them, too.

Then I saw me. Same old me. There I was, asleep in the back seat, and next to me was Meredith, also fast asleep.

We'd been away for the day, by the look of it. I wondered where we'd gone. Somewhere nice I dare say, somewhere special, maybe a treat somewhere. Yes. It had been Alton Towers, by the look of it. I was fast asleep with a paper hat on, and Alton Towers was written on the peak.

Maybe it had been their idea – the witches. Maybe they knew about the spell, the one which could only work on February 29th. Maybe they'd hoped to be out all day and not get back until after midnight.

Well, they'd got that wrong, just a little bit. There were still twenty-four minutes left. (Twenty-four minutes? Was that *all*?)

We watched from the shadows. We stood under a tree in next-door's garden and we watched, Meredith and I, almost – well – spellbound.

The car stopped in the driveway with a crunch of gravel. Dad opened the car door and said something to Mum which I couldn't quite hear. Then they went to the back of the car to wake the sleepy girls up. Meredith opened her eyes and rubbed them, then got out of the car and headed for the house.

But I didn't. I must have been too tired. So Dad reached in and undid my seat belt, and he slipped one hand under me, and one around me, and he lifted me from the car and carried me towards the house. Just like he used to do, when I was me, in the old days. And I saw that as he carried me, I half woke, and I reached up and put my arms around his neck.

Just like I'd always done.

And it all but broke my heart.

Then the front door closed behind me, and they had all gone inside. I felt like crying, but it was no time for tears. It was time for action. There were things to be done.

'Got the wool?'

'Here.'

Meredith took the three balls of golden wool from her pockets. One for me, one for her, one for spare.

'Come on.'

We crept into the garden, still keeping to the shadows so that we wouldn't be seen. Lights were going on and off inside the house, as those inside moved from quick drinks of milk in the kitchen, to hands and faces and teeth-brushing in the bathroom, to putting pyjamas on, to getting into bed, to asking for hot-water bottles, to the downstairs lights going on again.

We tied the ends of our balls of wool together and wound part of the wool around the front doorknob to anchor it, then we set off to encircle the house. Meredith went one way, I went the other.

I looked at my watch. Not long now. Under ten minutes to go.

I ducked down low as I came to the kitchen, staying well under the window. Once past the kitchen, I straightened up and rubbed my back.

Bang!

There was a sudden noise. I turned, startled. But it was only Spats – our cat. He'd come barging out of the cat flap to see what the night had to offer.

Wool, apparently.

He took one look at me, leapt up, and knocked the ball of wool from my hands. The next thing I knew he was tearing round the garden with it, getting it entangled in the rose bushes and winding it round the trees.

'Spats! Spats!' I hissed. 'Stop it!'

No good. He was running round the shed with it now, entangling himself in knots.

'Carly!'

It was Meredith. She'd been round the house with her wool and had come to meet me halfway.

'The cat! It's got the wool! Look at it! It's a complete nightmare! We'll never get it right, now!'

'Break it. We'll use the spare.'

I broke the wool. Spats ran off into another garden, trailing slivers of gold behind him which glinted in the moonlight.

We took the spare ball of wool and tied it to the other pieces.

'That's it now,' Meredith said. 'The unbroken golden circle.'

'What next?'

'The time and the spell. We have to wait. The spell has to be completed between the first stroke of midnight and the last. Only how will we know—?'

'We'll hear the church clock,' I said. 'Just listen.'

Which is what we did. We stood in the cold and the darkness and we listened. There was silence. Complete and utter silence. Then I heard my mum and dad's voices calling, 'Good night, Meredith. Good night Carly.'

I almost answered them.

Then a bedroom light went off. Then there was

the sound of two girls whispering. Their voices were faint, but the night was so still that even their whispering carried through the open window. The voice I heard was mine.

'Not long now,' I heard myself saying.

'Not long at all,' Meredith's voice replied. 'I'll soon have been in this body for thirteen months and weeks and days, to the very minute. And it'll be mine for ever! And all my glorious powers will come back! And when they do—'

'We can soon sort out *these* creeps!'

'Mumsy and Dadsy. Ha! All that lovey-dovey stuff. It makes you sick.'

'Turns your stomach.'

'I wonder what I should do to them?'

'I don't really mind what it is, as long as it's something very, very unpleasant.'

'Hey, sister, do you ever wonder about our old bodies?'

'In the Old Folks' home! Tee, hee, hee!'

'Do you think they're dead yet?'

'Wouldn't be surprised. Dead or gaga. Still, rather them than me.'

'My feelings exactly.'

'Night, then.'

'Night.'

And then something awful happened.

A cloud came over the moon. The spell wouldn't work if the moon wasn't visible. It wouldn't work. It wouldn't *work*!

Boonnnggg!

The first stroke of midnight rang.

But it was too late. No good. All for nothing. The

247

moon was hidden. The spell wouldn't work. All this
way, all this effort, all this trying and hoping. All for
nothing. We were defeated, done, it was over. The
witches had won. We would be old for ever now. Or
maybe not for ever. Not for much longer at all. We
would die soon, simply not be here, and maybe that
would be best.

I felt so sad. So sad. Yet resigned, too. It was over.
I'd tried my best to win my life back, but I had failed.
I had lost and they had won. Good didn't always win.
That was the truth of it. Sometimes evil did triumph
in the end. My life was over. I'd hardly lived it, and it
was gone.

The second chime of midnight rang. It rang clearly
through the chill night air, in the bleakness of the late
winter night.

'I'm sorry, Meredith, so sorry.'

'Me too, Carly, me too.'

I hugged my friend in my old arms. My special
friend. The sister I had never really had.

The third chime of midnight rang. So crisp, so
clear, it echoed in the starlight. So—

Then a miracle happened. A true and honest
miracle. Some gust of wind blew the cloud away from
the moon. It shone as clear as a beacon and as bright
as a lighthouse.

'Carly, the spell, quick!'

I grabbed the book, fumbling for the right page.
Hadn't I turned the page corner down? Why hadn't I
had the book at the ready? Oh, where, where, where?

I found it.

'Together, Meredith. Let's say it together.'

The fourth stroke of midnight rang. The bell tolled

out, as if summoning the dead to wake from their graves. We read out the spell.

> *'Within the golden band there lies*
> *The one that I would be*
> *My body and my soul exchange,*
> *And set my spirit free.*
> *For I would now be young again*
> *As I once used to be*
> *So let me be the one I name,*
> *And let that one be me.'*

And then we named them
'Carly!' I said.
'Meredith!'
And then—
—Nothing. Nothing happened. The bells rang on. They rang on, tolling out midnight, but slowly now it seemed, slower and slower, as if the day was running down, as though there were no energy left in it, and it was about to stop.

It didn't even seem to have the strength left to ring out the last seconds of midnight.

Bonnnngggg!

Another toll of the bell. It didn't sound so far away now, but long and loud, as if coming from just over your shoulder. It was as if time itself were creeping nearer, tiptoeing through the shadows, coming to claim you.

I looked at the old lady standing next to me. She was looking up towards a window. I looked too. And I saw them. The witches, in our bodies. Carly and Meredith. They were there at the bedroom window, staring down at us, their faces contorted with a whole mixture of emotions, with fear and rage and surprise and disbelief. They knew. Maybe they had heard our voices. But they knew that the spell had been said, that the circle had been completed, that everything had been done in the right way, and at the right time, by the light of the full moon, on the leap year day, between the first and the last chimes of midnight.

And it was all too late.

'No!' I saw myself shriek. 'No, no, no!'

Bonggggg!

The bell rang again. Was that for the twelfth time now? I couldn't say. I had lost count. I watched, transfixed, my feet like lead, my body suddenly so heavy, and so old. Not just ordinary old, but old with the weight of all the centuries, old with all the time and all the lifetimes that those witches had stolen and had lived.

But I felt something else too. It was almost as if a cheer went up from somewhere, from all those who had been robbed and tricked and who had lost their youth and their lives to these witches over the years.

A breeze gusted. The grass rustled.

'Yes,' it seemed to whisper. 'Yes, yes. At last, yes. Come join us now, come join us. We've been waiting for this moment for such a long time. Come join us. We're ready for you. We've been waiting, to be revenged.'

Bonnnnnggggg!

That had to be the last one, surely. The last chime of midnight. Or had time itself gone wrong? Was the church clock ringing thirteen? No. It wasn't

250

possible – was it? But then, what was and what wasn't possible now? Anything and everything.

'Look—' she said, the old lady next to me. Something was happening, to the two girls at the window, something was leaving them, flowing away from them, like the dust of angels. So faint, so fragile, almost like the makings of a distant rainbow. And then suddenly the ring of golden thread turned into a bright ring of fire, and it burnt with a golden flame, like a candle at an altar.

And something was happening to me, too. I was spinning around, like a little paper boat in a great whirlpool. Round and round, down and down, and I wasn't strong enough to swim against the motion. Nor did I want to. And yet I did. Instinctively, unable to stop myself I fought against going, against abandoning this familiarity and being torn away to – who knew what?

To the terrible unknown.

What if there was no destination at the end of this journey? What if I should be damned for ever, never to have a body again, to float amongst the clouds and the storms, looking down upon a world I could never be a part of?

And then there was a great blackness. Not the blackness of night, when you cannot make out the shapes in your room. But a complete and total blackness. The kind of blackness there must be when you have no eyes to see.

Nor hands to feel. Nor breath to take. No nose to smell, nor tongue to taste.

And then!

Then, then, then!

I was young.

I was *young*!

Light as a feather and free as a bird. Nimble as a grasshopper, swift as a swallow. I was out of the whirlpool and back on dry land. Perched on a high place, looking down at a scene.

The scene was a moonlit garden. But clouds were slowly covering the moon. Standing next to me was a tall girl, dark-haired and as graceful as a willow. And beneath us, in that moonlit garden, were two old women. Not nice old women, not sweet old ladies, but the ugliest, most repulsive hags you had ever seen.

Their faces were contorted in hatred and rage. They cursed and swore at us in ancient tongues, their voices harsh and guttural, their arms extended, their fingers crooked and pointing. They cursed and cursed as the last chime of midnight faded and disappeared into the remnants of yesterday.

It was a new day now. It was tomorrow. Tomorrow was today and yesterday was lost for ever, just dust blowing in the wind.

'Look,' Meredith said. 'Look!'

I could do nothing else. I couldn't move my eyes away.

The witches were growing older, before our very eyes. Older and uglier, great warts and carbuncles and blisters and boils appearing on their faces. Their hands became so gnarled and claw-like they closed in on themselves and turned into shapeless lumps on the ends of their arms, like stumps, like clubs.

'It's catching up with them,' I said, my voice just a whisper, 'all the time they ever lived. It's catching up

252

with them now. You can't cheat time – not in the end.'

Then the witches began to curve over; their backs turned into humps; their faces looked towards the ground. Their cries grew louder. Their curses and imprecations changed to wails of despair and pleas for help. But who could help them now?

They fell to their knees, almost as if in prayer. I could only see the tops of their heads and their faces, half hidden in shadow.

They seemed to have no flesh on them any more. We were looking down at skulls, at skeletons. And then there was a great *whoosh*! As if someone had sent a fresh breeze to blow the cobwebs from the world.

And I saw that they were dust.

Just dust. Nothing more. Two small piles of clothes, two pairs of elderly ladies' sensible shoes.

And dust.

The breeze took it and blew it away into the night. It danced away with it, two little swirling pillars of dust, into the darkness.

Then they were gone.

And it was over.

And all that was left of them were some old clothes in the garden, two small bundles of jumble sale rags.

'Meredith!'

'Carly!'

I hugged her for joy.

'Let me look at you!'

'Let me look at you!'

'You're so young!'

'And you! We're young again. We're young, we're young, we're young.'

We were young. We were ourselves. We were children. We were what we wanted to be, what we should have been. Once again we were the proud possessors of something that not all the wealth and the riches in the world can ever buy.

Youth. And childhood.

We were young again. And happy. Oh, so happy, we cried for joy.

20

Back

'What are you two up to? You should both be in bed!'

It was Dad.

I ran from the window and grabbed him in both of my arms. I held him tight enough to strangle him and I wouldn't let him go.

'Oh, Dad, Dad, Dad! Dad, Dad, Dad! It's so good to see you. It is, it is. I can't believe it. I can't. I can't believe I'm back here. In my own house, in my own room. I can't believe you're here. And that you've still got all your fingers!'

He seemed a bit bewildered.

'Em, yes, well, obviously I'm – I'm always delighted to see you too, Carly, only – I did – well – only just say goodnight to you a few minutes ago. So it hasn't really been all that long, has it?'

'Oh, Dad, I just want you to know that it's so wonderful to see you, it really is, and I still love you lots and lots. Even if you did stick me in a home. But I forgive you anyway. For that and for not believing me.'

'Pardon? Yes, well, it's always very nice of you to be so affectionate, and of course I love you lots and lots as well, Carly – and Meredith too, naturally, that all goes without saying. But it is actually bedtime!'

I still hung on to him and wouldn't let him go. Meredith came over from the window and give him a hug as well. Only I had hold of most of him, so she had to hug his leg.

'Oh, it's so good to see you, Mr Taylor!' she said. 'And thank you for taking me in and letting me stay, and for giving me a home.'

'Em – yes – well, that's all right, Meredith – and it's "John", remember? "Shelley" and "John". Not Mr and Mrs Taylor. Hardly any need to be formal after all this time.'

Then Mum came in.

'What's going on? What's all the commotion about?' She looked at Dad with disapproval. 'John! What are you doing? This is no time for horseplay and for messing about. We're had a long day and it's very late, and you should be letting Carly and Meredith get to sleep – not winding them up like this.'

'*Me?*' Dad wailed. 'It wasn't me! I only came in to see why they weren't in—'

'Mum, Mum, Mum!'

I let go of Dad and raced across the room.

'Mum, I'm back,' I said. 'We're both back. Me and Meredith, we're ourselves again. This is her. The real Meredith. You've never met her before, have you? Not the real one!'

And I gave Mum a hug, too.

She didn't seem all that pleased to get hugged though.

'Carly, what are you talking about? What are you doing? What do you mean, the real Meredith? Honestly, what's got into everyone. If this is what's going to happen every time we go out for the day, we'd better just stay at home in future.'

'I wouldn't mind, Mum,' I said. 'Not at all. I'd be happy to stay at home for ever! In fact I don't think I ever want to go anywhere else again.'

'Carly, Meredith – it's very late.'

And then—

'What's *that*?' Dad said. He was at the window. Looking down into the back garden, at the two small piles of old clothes lying there. 'Look at that. Someone's chucked a load of old jumble over the fence. I'd better go and—'

'Not now, John, please,' Mum said, trying unsuccessfully to prise me off her. 'Leave it till the morning. It's far too late. We must all get to bed.'

And then I felt so hugely and so suddenly tired, so utterly and absolutely exhausted, that I had to agree.

So we all said goodnight, and Meredith got into her bed, and I got into mine. And I fell asleep in my own bed, for the first time in ages. But not simply in my own bed. In my own body as well.

In the morning, the clothes had gone from the garden. I stretched and yawned and poked Meredith to wake up and see. She stretched and yawned too.

Then we got dressed – in young clothes – and went down for breakfast.

There should have been repercussions of course. Lots of them. But somehow they didn't materialize.

I expected someone to come round from the Merrysides Home for Retired and Elderly Gentlefolk to say that Meredith's granny had gone missing.

But they never did. Maybe Mrs Horrington just couldn't be bothered. Maybe she was just glad that the two old ladies had run away together, as it meant she could put the rent up and let their room out to somebody else. Possibly three old ladies this time, or even four. It wouldn't have surprised me to learn that she'd got bunk beds in, and was stacking old ladies in one on top of another, like sardines. She'd probably told Nurse Bartley and the other residents that we'd gone off to stay with relatives, so as to stop them asking any awkward questions.

Then there were the clothes. Had Dad picked the clothes up and thrown them away? If so, why hadn't he said?

And then there was the book, the ancient book with the metal clasp and 'Necromancy' on the cover in faded gold leaf. What had become of that book of spells? Had it crumbled into dust too, along with the witches? Or had it burst into flames with the circle of gold? I never knew, and I never saw it again. Maybe it had it fallen into other hands. If it had, I hoped they were good ones.

I did. I truly did.

And then there was me. My body was older than it had been when I had left it. I'd missed all those lessons at school, too. I didn't know half the stuff I was supposed to.

Neither did Meredith. Our marks were terrible and the teachers wondered what was wrong. There were even some new children in the class as well, who'd started after Christmas, and we didn't know who they were. It was as if we'd lost our memories.

Mum and Dad got very worried about us and took

us to the doctor. He couldn't find anything wrong though. So then Mum thought we were just acting up deliberately and pretending to have forgotten everything we ought to know just to annoy everybody, as if it were some kind of practical joke.

Some joke.

Then she took us to a child psychologist, who told us to think of her as a friend and to tell us all our problems. But when I said I didn't have any thank you very much, as all my problems had now been solved (at least the big ones had). She just said, 'Hmm!' and peered at me through her glasses and made notes on her notepad and then said, 'Very interesting'.

Then she told Mum that we were suffering from 'collective amnesia' whatever that was, and that there was nothing to be done, but to bear with it until it wore off.

Well, we soon caught up on the lessons we'd missed and everything else, and we were pretty much back to normal.

All the while though I kept on wondering if I ought to tell Mum and Dad the truth, about what had *really* happened and where I'd *really* been and how I'd been stolen by the witches, and how the person they thought had been me had really been a witch.

I asked Meredith what she thought.

'I don't suppose there's any harm in trying, Carly,' she said. 'But I don't think anyone will believe you. They'll never believe us. No one will. At least I don't think so. But you try, if you like, and I'll back you up if your mum asks me. But I'm just glad to be me again and to have a home and to have you as my friend. I'm content to leave it at that.'

My chance came one afternoon. Mum was alone in the kitchen, reading the newspaper. I'd come in to get a drink. I felt her watching me. I turned to meet her gaze. She smiled.

'You've changed, you know, Carly,' she said.

'Oh,' I said. 'Have I?'

'Yes,' she said. 'You're more like you used to be, when you were younger.'

'In what way, Mum?'

'Warmer. Kinder. I don't know – more like *you*. These last couple of months, you sometimes seemed so – so different. It was almost as if I didn't know you. Almost as if you were somebody else. Even your handwriting seemed to have changed. But now you're more like your old self again. Oh, I don't know – I'm probably imagining it. Anyway – as long as you're happy.'

'Perfectly, Mum,' I said.

And I was.

And I am. And I left it at that. I decided not to tell her.

I've got red hair and freckles and my name is Carly – although it's Scarlet really, only I call myself Carly to tone down the red hair a little and not draw attention to it.

I've got a few podgy bits, but they're not as podgy as they once were. I suppose I'm growing up.

I don't mind the red hair so much any more. In fact I might go back to calling myself Scarlet again.

I live with my mum and dad and my adopted sister Meredith, who as well as being my adopted sister is also my best friend. We rarely quarrel. We get on really well. I used to have a real sister once, but she was only with us a little while. The name we gave her was Marsha, and she was perfect in every way. And when we lost her she left us feeling lonely, and things were never the same.

So my chance came. But I didn't take it. I didn't tell Mum about the witches, about how I was stolen, about my life as an old lady, about how I escaped and became myself again.

Meredith was right. She would never have believed me. And why should she? It's not a story I would have believed either, if someone had told it to me.

'Stolen!' I'd have said. 'Oh yeah! Witches! Oh sure! Pull the other one. It's got bells on. That kind of thing's just for kids!'

But it's another world, you see. Grown-ups forget. Because they *have* grown up. It all goes away from them, and they can't remember it any more, not the magic, nor the wonder, nor the mystery, nor the fear.

It'll happen to me one day.

I'll grow up too. And tell myself not to be so silly. And maybe not even believe my own story, and deny my own truth.

But I'll try not to. I really will. But who knows? Who knows what time can do?

I'll tell you one thing, though. Sometimes, at the end of our street, down by the shops, where the boys and girls gather when there's nothing to do, sometimes they tease the old people, as they walk past.

But I never do. I tick them off if I see that happening. They think it's just because of my red hair – and that it means I've got a fiery temper.

I haven't though. That's not true. It's just that I

understand what they don't understand; I've seen what they haven't seen, and I know what they don't know.

Inside every old lady, you see, there could be a young girl, slim and pretty and agile, calling to her friends. Inside of every old man, there could be a young boy, with a skateboard at his feet.

Maybe they watch hungrily, as the children around them play and laugh and run and kick footballs and do handstands and spin round in cartwheels.

Maybe they watch longingly, remembering when they too were young, only a short while, a few brief moments ago.

Maybe their lives were stolen by witches and they never got them back. You never know. Maybe they're hoping, maybe they're waiting, for the time to be right. Just as I was. Waiting for someone to discover the spell, which will make them young again.

So I always try to be kind, if I can, to all the old people I see.

Because you never know.

Never.

They're probably just as young as you are, inside, where it counts.

No, you never really know, you see. You never really know.

About anyone.

Not anyone in the whole wide world.

THE GREAT BLUE YONDER

'You'll be sorry when I'm dead.'

That's what Harry said to his sister, before the incident with the lorry. And now he is just that – dead.

And he wishes more than anything that he hadn't said it. He wishes he could say sorry. And say goodbye to everyone he left behind – his mum, his dad, his best friend Pete, even Jelly Donkins, the class bully.

Now he's on the Other Side, waiting to move on to the Great Blue Yonder. But he doesn't know how to get there – until he meets Arthur, a small boy in a top hat, who's been dead for years, who helps him say goodbye . . .

THE SPEED OF THE DARK

The speed of the dark is the heart of a nightmare.

A snow dome – and a broken one at that – was a strange thing to find nailed to anyone's desk. Especially the desk of Chris Mallan, a scientist with a mysterious past. Chris has one mission in life – to invent the impossible. A 'decelerator' that can slow the speed of light to a point where it turns to darkness. To a point where matter is made miniature.

Then Chris himself disappears. Leaving behind nothing except the dome – and his life story. A story so bizarre it surely can't be believed. About an artist with a fiendish skill. An imprisonment that can never end. And a boy who gives everything he has to find the people he loves.

A selected list of titles available from Macmillan Children's Books

The prices shown below are correct at the time of going to press. However, Macmillan Publishers reserve the right to show new retail prices on covers which may differ from those previously advertised.

All Macmillan titles can be ordered from our website, www.panmacmillan.com, or from your local bookshop and are available by post from:

Bookpost
PO Box 29, Douglas, Isle of Man IM99 1BQ

Credit cards accepted. For details:
Telephone: 01624 836000
Fax: 01624 670923
E-mail: bookpost@enterprise.net
www.bookpost.co.uk

Free postage and packing in the UK.
Overseas customers: add £1 per book (paperback)
and £3 per book (hardback).